Anna and Sebastian

by
Marlene Lee

STEPHEN F. AUSTIN STATE UNIVERSITY PRESS

Production Manager: Kimberly Verhines
Book Design: Mallory LeCroy
Cover Art: The Barbara Hepworth Museum and Sculpture Garden, St Ives,
Cornwall, UK. Two Forms (Divided Circle), 1969, bronze

IBSN: 978-1-62288-257-1

For more information:
Stephen F. Austin State University Press
P.O. Box 13007 SFA Station
Nacogdoches, Texas 75962
sfapress@sfasu.edu
936-468-1078

Distributed by Texas A&M University Press Consortium
www.tamupress.com

CONTENTS

For Margaret and Jerry Norton, cherished friends.

Chapter One

Daylight through the drapes. Early birdsong. The silence before doors slam and engines start up.

Wait. Was this her bedroom? Or the hospital room? Was she merely remembering birdsong or actually hearing it?

She waited for the equipment on the hospital roof to kick in—a heating and cooling unit?—its first throbs rattling windows, disturbing the top-story weather and light.

But there was no throbbing. No machinery.

She was back home on Woodland Street.

Out of bed slowly, leaning on her cane. Into the kitchen for the final pot of coffee, last newspaper delivery. Front page scan. Immediately after, the trek through accidents, arrests, fires, obituaries.

Sebastian. Another disappearance.

When she was younger and in good health, she didn't mind his absences. Through the years, few telephone calls. He'd never had a landline or owned a cell phone. It took him days to learn about her accident. But when he wanted to find her, he did. Now that she was leaving 915 Woodland Street, she considered putting a card in the window of the front door, *vacated business*. But she had limits. Twice she'd laid down those limits and been surprised. Like a grave old dog carrying his own leash, Sebastian had come back. Still, if she kept the figurative leash taut, hooked it to a doorknob or bedpost, he would chew through it and waste no time in disappearing again.

Chapter Two

Anna waited inside her empty house for the van. Staring into the bare bookcases and clean, dead fireplace, she felt the absence of heirlooms: the desk where she'd written her textbook. The generations-old rocking chair. Her grandparents' two-leaf mahogany dining table. Parents' matching Hickock chairs. She almost felt disturbed dust of the old brick house sifting into cracks between floorboards.

When the doorbell chimed she rose and stepped out into—what?

From the back seat of the van, its panels stamped with The Oaks Retirement Center, she watched eighty years in this neighborhood roll by like a film scene. Her heart rate controlled every close-up, every horizontal pan.

Emerging from Woodland Street, the van approached a new roundabout, installed since she'd stopped driving a year ago; no, since she'd been *stopped* from driving a year ago. The new circle was built as a result of the accident—her fault—in which she pulled out into traffic. The collision replays itself every time she rides in a car. Her concussion and broken legs were nothing compared to the post-accident tremor that has eroded her confidence, not to mention her grasp of everything from silverware to complex ideas. The driver of the other car was killed.

"How d'you like these roundabouts?" asked the young driver of the van over his shoulder. "One more change to get used to."

"That's life, isn't it, one change after another," she said absently. As they entered the roundabout, she closed her eyes to block out the looming hood of the black SUV bearing down on her. Nothing, however, could dull the shriek of metal stuck like shrapnel in her memory. A familiar thought circulated tiredly: why should someone in the larger, heavier car be killed while she, in her little Cooper, was spared?

At The Oaks her cane steadied her. The driver setting her suitcase onto the elevator made her feel, if not less alone, at least temporarily attended. At the door of her apartment she found the keyhole. The bolt shot back and she opened the door. Here, she was safe.

Until now she had not lived to be safe. She'd taken risks, marrying the man she loved, Lorenzo, a Black man, rejected by her parents, rejected by many others, and though the marriage had ended in his death and their daughter's death, she was grateful for both marriage and child.

She'd intended to carry the suitcase into the bedroom but, instead, found herself sitting in the rocking chair, perhaps even dozing, though she tried to guard against these shallow naps. Outside, the canopy of oak trees brushed against the fifth-story window of her new living room.

"Aunt Anna?"

She hadn't heard the knock. Nahum, remnant of her marriage to Lorenzo, stepped over the threshold. Kind of heart. African American. Assistant director of The Oaks. Nahum was why she was here.

"Nahum!"

"Aunt Anna." In the brimming quietude that was her nephew, he bent over her, straightened, and gently swung her hands in his. "I've been waiting for you."

While they talked about her arrival, the underlying wordlessness was about each other. *How are you? No, I mean how are you really?* Nahum broke eye contact to look at his aunt's new home. Paintings he'd known since boyhood. Piano. Small Persian rugs laid down here and there over standard carpeting. Lighted table lamps in the dusky afternoon.

Curious, she thought, how a splinter of family firmed her up. But as inexplicably as it came, the moment ended. Later, after he left, she continued rocking until the room he'd transformed felt surreal again, not yet hers. She walked into the bedroom to unpack her suitcase.

Chapter Three

That evening, entering The Oaks dining room, she was met by a couple named Meg and Philip who introduced themselves as her neighbors. They'd arranged for her to sit at their table where Anna made an effort to converse interestingly while not dropping her fork. As the three of them tried to bridge the gap between their work lives—Meg and Philip's car dealership, Anna's career on the law faculty at the university—she glanced among the linen-covered tables scattered throughout the dining room. Everyone was old, apparently prosperous, and white as the tablecloths.

"—the art market in Florida was booming back then," a man at the next table was saying, sharing his life story with several women whose attentions, Anna thought, fluttered around him like moths bumping against a porch light. "I never told a client *I don't know how to do*"—he gestured wittily—"*such-and-such*. I either learned or subcontracted it out..."

After dinner, in the Fireside Room, she accepted a brandy from her new neighbors' private supply.

"I have no idea where my daughters got their talent and brains," said a woman in purple sitting at the built-in bar running along one side of the room. "Certainly not from me."

"From your husband, then?" suggested her friend, a slim woman with a smoker's parchment skin.

"Probably not. My husband is no more intelligent or talented than I am."

"I resemble that remark," said her husband, coming up behind her and resting his hand on the purple expanse. He turned and winked at Anna who smiled and sipped her Cognac.

These evenings would be spent listening to people talk about their pasts, their children, their grandchildren. With luck she might hear an occasional ironic remark, something with a bite to it, like the self-assessment just delivered by the woman in purple.

During the next few days Anna sampled the café, lunch room, formal dining room, exercise room, library, two film showings, a meeting of the book club, a trip to the mall. By Sunday morning she was too tired to accept her new neighbors' invitation to join them for the religious service. Anyway, she was not a churchgoer. Her religion was reading; her Sunday worship service was the newspapers.

"May I join you for dinner, though?" she asked. "In fact, why don't you drop by my apartment before we go down to the dining room together."

But by late afternoon Anna found herself tired all over again as well as discouraged. The Sunday papers left her feeling walled off from a world where headlines popped and interesting people engaged in news-worthy activities. With sudden, frightening intensity, she loathed her new home. Contemplating drinks with Meg and Philip left her feeling not only bored but actually hostile toward her nice new neighbors.

How was she to pass the time here? Oh, and by the way, what was her purpose in living? Even while she fretted, she knew that the underlying question, the ragged hole at the center, had less to do with moving into a retirement center or fulfilling a purpose than with the disappearance of Sebastian. Why had she not heard from him? Where had he gone?

At 5:30, Anna carried appetizers into the living room as if rounds of toast spread with brie could make up for cold detachment.

"Sunday brunch is one of our favorite occasions in the week," Meg said as Philip mixed drinks at the pass-through kitchen counter. "The Oaks provides a wonderful buffet."

"We pay for it on Sunday nights, though," said Philip. "It's lean pickin's tonight."

"Are you on the weekly or monthly meal plan, Anna?" Meg asked.

"Weekly," said Anna, wondering if she should change to the month-ly plan, which allowed some meals to be taken alone in the apartment. "The van doesn't drive people to restaurants, does it?"

"No," said Meg, "but I can see why. It's really against The Oaks' interest. They want us to eat here in the dining room."

"They could make an occasional restaurant run," Anna suggested, "without undermining their business plan."

"If you give people an inch, they'll take a mile," said Philip, handing around drinks. "They'd want the van to take them to every grandchild's recital and school event in town."

"The profit motive," Anna said. Meg and Philip stared. Trying to correct what must have sounded to them like a strange remark, she added, "They have to pay for gasoline and the driver, I suppose. It all adds up."

Philip shrugged and seated himself. "Of course it all adds up. That's why they don't do it."

Philip's "lean pickin's" remark proved to be accurate. As they stood in line for Sunday night left-overs, Anna saw the plain woman in purple, though today it was chartreuse, join the buffet line carrying a large basket and thermos. Behind her came her husband and another couple, all laughing.

"Looks like the Radcliffes are having another picnic," said Meg.

"Isn't it a little chilly for a picnic?" said Anna.

"Oh, The Oaks has a sunroom with tables and a lovely fountain," said Meg. "We can bring the great outdoors inside year-round."

Anna realized she'd hardly been outside since she stepped into The Oaks days earlier. A welcoming bouquet of hothouse roses from The Oaks management had been her last contact with nature. Somewhere she owned a picnic basket. And somewhere there was a large thermos bottle, probably in the basement storage unit. But retrieving them felt like an exhausting prospect.

Was she physically unable to have a picnic? Or did she simply not want to go to the trouble? Neither a sunroom's captured warmth nor the plash of a fountain could overcome her inertia. Even the approach of spring failed to interest her. She mourned the disappearance of pleasure.

Chapter Four

Anna was engaged in a quiet rant at the breakfast table. "It should have been called *Oratorio for War* instead of *Oratorio for Peace.* The brass and drums were very, very loud. And photograph slides of war victims were gratuitous. Ultimately sentimentalized." Outrage left her more cheerful and sure of herself than she'd felt in a week.

"How was the music?" asked Meg.

"Mundane."

"How were the choir and soloists?" asked Philip.

"Good. But when all was said and done, the concert insulted one's intelligence. I came home dispirited. Deception is everywhere."

Meg and Philip looked baffled.

"The music wasn't honest," Anna continued, "and the graphic images certainly weren't."

"How can photographs be dishonest?" asked Philip. "Assuming they haven't been doctored."

Seeing that her criticism was beginning to attract attention around the breakfast table, Anna modulated her voice. "The slides sensationalized war. Gore and suffering were flashed on the screen again and again. It was an excuse to view horror without actually living through it." She shivered. "And there was the constant noise of the trumpets and trombones and drums. Peace got top billing, but war high-jacked the music." *Listen to the bugles,* she thought. *Thrill to the snare drums. Watch the children die in the streets. And it's called an oratorio for peace.*

That afternoon the woman who had recycled her wardrobe back to the purple pantsuit said, "I couldn't help overhearing you at breakfast." They were standing in the mailroom off the lobby. Anna had learned that her name was Georgina.

"I apologize for ranting," said Anna, "though I think these hypocrisies need to be aired."

"I thought you were magnificent," said Georgina. Then, "What are hypocrisies?"

"Lies that don't sound like lies," said Anna. She cocked her head. "No, that's not quite right. Something that, on the surface, seems true but actually means the opposite."

"Like ads that say you can lose thirty pounds in a week?"

"Well, those are outright lies," said Anna. "No, something that claims to be about peace but actually excites us to war." She searched for an example. "Hypocrisy would be a magazine that shows a thin woman on the cover and photographs of glossy desserts when you turn the page."

Georgina snorted. "Just about every magazine does that."

Anna liked a woman who could snort, and the purple pantsuit was bracing. As if on cue, they both pulled out advertising brochures from their shiny brass mailboxes in the wall.

"Is this what we're talking about?" said Georgina.

Anna dropped her circular in the wastebasket. "We're surrounded by nonsense."

"Our daughter is a commercial artist," said Georgina. "She has serious talent but she has to earn a living, so she puts together ads like these."

Anna nodded sympathetically. "People would rather buy electronic shampoo than original art."

"What's electronic shampoo?" Georgina asked, interested.

"Just something I made up."

Georgina's plain face surprised Anna by its sudden wistful expression. "If my daughter could make a living from her sculpted figures..." She trailed off.

A daughter, thought Anna. *How profoundly wonderful to have an adult daughter.*

"That's how she describes her work," Georgina said. "She works in clay. She calls them sculpted figures. Well," she said, waving away wistfulness, "I'm off for my afternoon nap. Nice talking to you."

Anna nodded absently. She'd never been able to take a satisfying nap. How pleasant it would be to wake up in the afternoon refreshed. Instead, she dozed in the rocking chair, startled into wakefulness by a dry mouth, stiff joints, and dark visions from restless hypnagogues.

Carrying two newspapers, a magazine, and an envelope that at first made her reel backward because she briefly mistook it for a letter from Sebastian, she proceeded down the hall. Nahum's office door was closed. The chaplain's, though, was open.

Looking up, he said, "Good morning, Mrs. Orland."

She smiled. "It's Ms.," she said, and continued on to the elevators.

Chapter Five

Sebastian didn't like to be tied to a schedule. If Anna planned a dinner or wanted to see a movie, it had been easier to do it by herself. Sometimes they would drop in on people who self-selected as his friends, spontaneous people who could wing it when he called out of the blue: "Hey, can I come over tonight?" They knew how to say yes: "Sure, Sebastian. Come on over."

Sometimes she'd gone with him to the artists' and social activists' homes he favored. They probably found her too conventional, too mainstream. Forty years earlier—had she and Sebastian really been together forty years?—she couldn't bring herself to wear sandals, batik, go braless. As a matter of fact, she dressed more youthfully now than she had when she was young. Black tights, tunics, boots. Her haircut, though not actually spiky, was short on one side, longer and tucked behind her ear on the other. She wouldn't go so far as to color a forelock red or blue, but she *would* honor old age by keeping her hair white.

"Are you settling in?" Nahum asked as they passed through the lobby at the same time.

"Not quite yet," she said. It was her second week at The Oaks. "After a lifetime on Woodland Street..."

He smiled. "I remember playing with your dog—"

"Chappie," said Anna.

"And catching fireflies with the neighbor kids in the dark—"

"The Belden boys."

"And learning piano and guitar from Uncle Lorenzo."

Anna was unable to hear Lorenzo's name without a release of feeling that had never gone stale. She hadn't asked for a reminder of past happiness, all this fresh feeling, but a talent for staleness was a gift she'd never received.

Seeing the collapse in his aunt's face, Nahum moved closer.

"Oh, Nahum," she said into his shoulder, "I haven't heard from Sebastian in a very long time." She didn't cry but she did lean hard before bearing her own weight again.

Taking his aunt's face between his hands, Nahum said, "Sebastian will be back."

She bowed her head. "This time feels different."

"Because you've moved? Everything must feel different now. Come, have some coffee with me." He put an arm around her and guided her to the conference table in his office. "Does Sebastian know you're here?"

"I told him," said Anna. "I wrote down my new address long before I moved."

"I guess he still doesn't like to use the phone."

"Still doesn't like the phone."

Nahum smiled and shook his head. "Doesn't even own a cell phone, does he."

"Nope." Anna looked off into the distance. "Actually, I don't like cell phones, either."

"Nevertheless, you use one," said Nahum.

"Yes. Not the apps, though. Such an ugly word."

"Not very melodious," agreed Nahum. "I suppose you've considered reporting his absence to the police?"

"I've considered it, yes. Over the years I've considered it more than once and I've always been glad I didn't."

"Because he always comes back."

"I worry more than I used to," she said. During Nahum's tactful silence, Anna looked away. "You're thinking I choose to worry."

"Well," said Nahum considerately, "it's a pattern."

Slightly annoyed by the truth, she set her cup down with a sharp rap and changed the subject. "How's your family?"

"Fine. They say hi. We want you to come over some evening for dinner."

"I'm always glad to see you, Nahum." She stood and reached for a hug. "I wouldn't like to live here without you." On her way out of the office she added, "I'll wait a few more days before calling the police." But after all, she thought, that's what they're here for, to help. She proceeded down the hall and entered the elevator. So what if Sebastian doesn't need help? *I* need help.

Through the years some of her friends—two in particular, both dead now—had thought she needed help, as in counseling help, therapy help, because she loved a man who didn't want to be accountable to her. *Do you want to spend your life worrying about where Sebastian is and what he's doing?* they asked. *Your love life is neurotic, Anna,* they said. *You're settling for less than you deserve.* Nor, years earlier, had they understood why she married Lorenzo. Why not marry a White man, they said, like every other White woman we know? When little Marianna died, their grief went beyond sympathy; they themselves mourned the child. When Lorenzo died soon after, they understood Anna's desperate sadness. But with Sebastian, they drew the line.

She reached the fifth floor. Once again she decided not to report his absence to the police. But in all these years she hadn't learned not to worry; hadn't learned to accept his mysterious need for solitude. Perhaps her worrying was a way to entertain herself. As Nahum said, part of a pattern. Was Sebastian a kind of theatre for her? Was he a chance for her to step onstage and see herself in a drama? A rehearsal for something? Was Sebastian, too, rehearsing for something?

She entered the apartment and went to the window. If the limbs of the oaks bending and blowing in the early spring wind came any closer, they would scrape the glass. When she slid open the bedroom door to the balcony, the gust cleared her mind. For a few minutes there was nothing but brisk, chilly air and sunlight through rising and falling branches.

If she could have seen the scarf at her neck flutter, her white hair fly, the color in her face rise, she would have delighted in aliveness and wondered why she ever worried about anything. Marianna, Lorenzo, the driver of the black SUV, Sebastian, the inevitable rubbing out of the future, all were momentarily erased, blown aside, mysteriously still part of her, yet as natural as tree limbs, as weightless as space.

Chapter Six

Half dozing in her rocking chair the next afternoon, she once again felt—or heard?—the throbbing of the heating and cooling unit on the hospital roof. And was that a knock on the door?

She started. Flower delivery. Early tulips. Stems and flowers in a glass vase. Garlic-like bulbs submerged in a watery bubble at the bottom. They were from her Woodland Street neighbors. At the table by the window she half-buried her face in the forced blooms. Satiated, almost drunk on pinkness and giddy scent, she moved sluggishly back to the rocking chair.

She dozed and was startled awake again, this time by a stronger knock on her door. Between the time she lifted her head and uttered "Come in," a pleasant little frisson shot through her. When the door opened and Sebastian entered as if being here were the most ordinary thing in the world, she could have fainted from happiness.

"Anna." Offering his hand, he helped her up from the rocking chair. Through her brief spate of tears, he pulled her against him, took a step back, then drew her forward again. His cheek, slightly rough with new beard, stirred her. She passed through the familiar stages: joy, interest in his male strangeness, arousal. They walked arm in arm to the sofa.

"You're fine?" she finally said.

"Always okay."

As long as she'd known him, he was "always okay." When she first knew him, she'd had to guess how he really was. She still didn't quite know.

Sitting close, they absorbed as much of each other as they could, limited by the weeks apart.

"Have you been safe?" she asked. It was a silly question since safety was not a value either of them lived by. *Had* lived by. Anna was more willing to be safe now than ever before.

"I keep myself safe enough," he said. If he was ever in danger, she thought, he would be his own best friend.

He lifted her hand and touched it to his lips. "I've been gone longer than I wanted."

The wording caught her attention. "Longer than expected" is what he usually said, a neutral statement, not even interesting. "Longer than I wanted" suggested a problem. Loss of control. It was not like Sebastian.

"Oh?" she said.

With his free hand he reached for the magazine she'd recently brought upstairs. His craggy profile and wiry gray hair seemed alien in the room. Levi's and work shoes looked out of place in the—be honest—sterile apartment. The man was productive and needed a dense setting: pottery, music, clay, paints, brushes, food, ingredients, pots and pans.

"I haven't brought everything up from storage yet," she murmured, as if he'd said, *What are you doing in this sterile apartment, Anna?* They were both looking at one of his teapots resting alone on a shelf.

"It looks good there," he said, and used the comment as a chance to stand. "It's Asian in its simplicity." She loved him for describing something in her living room as beautiful, foreign, even philosophical.

He bent to the tulips, stems magnified by the glass. Long-legged, lean of hip, Sebastian intrigued her. He was otherness. Every time those competent hands wrapped themselves around wet clay at the wheel, she fell in love with him all over again. He was younger by eleven years.

"Over time I hope the apartment will feel like mine," she said. Neither of them mentioned 915 Woodland Street. The topic had been disposed of. "I can't take care of my home any longer," she'd said after the accident. "I can hardly climb stairs. My hands tremble, my balance..."

"I can help you," he'd said, and meant it, at least at the moment he spoke. But she knew he would not be happy coming at a preordained time to put out the garbage or be available to fetch what she needed from upstairs. He loved to cook, but he would not like planning and shopping for meals that seemed to come at alarming regularity. Meals seemed to rush toward her with shocking frequency. There was not enough time between eating and sleeping to read all that she wanted to read, update the textbook, play the piano, take slow walks outside.

He turned away from the tulips and returned to the sofa. "Well, old gal." They gazed at each other, familiar but also curious. *Has anything changed between us?* "How's The Oaks treating you?"

"Good. Nahum makes it easier."

"Do you see him every day?"

"No, but often." She reached up to push a lock of white hair back from his forehead. "How's Heather?"

"Heather's okay."

His eighteen-year-old daughter lived with him across the river where he rented space in the basement of a converted warehouse. The narrow windows of his studio looked out at sidewalk level. A pang of desire struck Anna. To be in his studio. To glance out the windows and watch feet and legs going by. To see Sebastian at the potter's wheel. She felt tethered to The Oaks.

In a sense, she'd always been tethered while Sebastian roamed free. She hadn't minded. She may even have liked it. Freedom for him was also freedom for her. She didn't think he loved any woman but her, but if, over the years, he *had* fallen for someone else, wouldn't she have noticed? As for herself, she'd loved him since they first met. Seated here beside her again, studying their hands resting together in her lap, he seemed to be waiting, not for her to say something, not for the walk into the bedroom that marked their reunions, but for something within himself, something that would guide him to the next step. He studied the single pottery teapot on the shelf.

Following his gaze, she asked, "Have you been working at the studio?" Unasked: *Why have you stayed away longer than you wanted to?*

"Yeah, but I didn't get much done." He turned and laid his hand at the base of her neck. Settling together, they kissed, then rose and walked into the bedroom. Silently they undressed. Side by side in bed, he said quietly, "She's going away."

"Who?"

"Heather."

Anna got up on one elbow.

"Chicago," he said, and turned his head sharply toward her on the pillow.

Anna lay back and stared at the ceiling. *Is this why you've stayed away longer than you wanted to?* Her breathing grew careful and shallow. "Are you moving to Chicago with her?"

"I don't think so," he said. Under the blankets he reached for her hand. "Did you bring the homeless pack?"

Of course she had. The homeless pack, as they called it—pajamas, clean socks, and underwear—rested on a closet shelf reserved for his things. On Woodland Street they'd called his shelf "the cubby," storage space for a preschooler. It amused Sebastian.

"An artist never grows up," he'd said, happy with the concept; happy that Anna set aside a place for him; happy, she realized, that he could come and go as he liked and there would always be clean socks.

Could she have written her textbook, a book used for years in law school classes, the book that assured her financial security, if she'd had a husband and children draining her attention through the years? A husband and children instead of a lover? "Draining" was not the word that came to mind when she'd been wife to Lorenzo and mother to Marianna. "Engrossed," perhaps. "Engaged." Ultimately the right word for that period in her life, she decided, was "happy." A simple word for a simple state.

The other word was "tired." Very tired. She remembered being so tired when Marianna was a baby that sleep seemed like the condition most necessary to life. More necessary than food. Yet she would welcome a lifetime of fatigue if she could have her daughter back. For her, Marianna's death was like a wound that never stopped bleeding. For Lorenzo, it was suicide. When he'd turned away for one casual moment and Marianna darted into traffic, love curdled into guilt and he was unable to live without their child.

Anna's center was tested then. Even now, the sediment of grief lay so thick she couldn't remember who she'd seen, what she'd done, whether or not she ate and slept. The only thing she could point to was the textbook she'd begun as a way to stay sane. For six years she wrote the book. It was published. She gained tenure. Gained a deanship. Returned to teaching. Ate. Slept. Read. Played piano. Retired. Ran a stop sign. Killed a person. Endured injuries. Frailty. The Oaks.

Through forty years there'd been Sebastian—here, not here, loved and loving. When he'd learned about the accident, he came to the hospital every day. He lived at Woodland Street for the weeks she'd been an invalid. After the healthcare aide left at one o'clock, he stayed with her through the afternoons and nights. She was, she learned, more than a convenient habit. He loved her.

Chapter Seven

Sebastian shopped for food and cooked meals in Anna's little kitchen at The Oaks. He could do chicken paprika just as well in "the galley," he called it, as he could in the big kitchen on Woodland Street. Anna's neighbors hardly saw him beyond brief introductions in the elevator. He *did* talk to the elegant, self-described artist of Florida renown.

"I met a great talker in the parking lot," he said one afternoon as he carried bags of groceries into the apartment. "A sculptor from Florida. Unafflicted by modesty. I couldn't get away. But the more I listened, the less I wanted to get away."

"I hear him almost every evening," Anna said. "Women love him."

"I didn't catch his name, though I learned the story of his life."

"Michel," said Anna.

"Michel," he said, delighted.

A week after Sebastian decamped from The Oaks, his daughter visited and said she wanted to meet Mike. *Who is that?* Anna wondered. Soon realizing that Sebastian had performed a progressive downgrade from "Michel" to "Mike," she took Heather to lunch where she could meet the man her father found interesting enough to rename.

Heather's planned move to Chicago went unmentioned as the two rode the elevator down to the dining room, absorbed, as they were, in the Michel/Mike mission. Anna spotted him at a table near the entrance already entertaining two handsome women whose musical laughter gave the dining room an air of *charme et gaieté*.

"May we join you?" she asked, and accepted his gallant offer of two vacant chairs at the table—*his* table, since, clearly, the table belonged to him.

"I see you have a visitor," he said, gesturing toward Heather. Even when stating the obvious, he had the air of someone whose ordinary words are merely a gateway to something extraordinary.

Heather extended her hand. "Heather. My father, Sebastian, met you a few days ago."

"In the parking lot, I believe," Anna said.

"Oh, yes. Yes. Certainly," said Michel. "How nice to meet you." Anna watched his charm kick in at the same time the autobiography resumed. "I was just saying that my wife and I opened a gallery in Miami..."

"Yes, I know," said Heather. "My father told me."

Unabashed, he leaned forward—"I understand your father is an artist?"—including both Anna and the two women in his question, although Sebastian could not possibly have been Anna's father.

"He is," said Heather, and wasted no time focusing him on what interested her. "Are you familiar with Chicago, sir?"

"Not at all." Michel leaned back in his chair as the waitress delivered luncheon plates.

"I'm moving there," Heather said. "I thought you might know something about the city."

"'Fraid not," said Michel, startling Anna by sounding both Midwestern and modest at the same time. "I'm strictly Floridian."

"How did you happen to come here to Missouri?" asked one of the women.

"That makes for an interesting story," said Michel. "New Yorkers were retiring to Miami in droves and they all needed art for their second homes..."

The narrative reached the point where his wife had grown ill, the sale of the Miami gallery was accomplished, they'd come to Missouri to be near her adult children, she died, he'd been stunned—"'beached,' to use a Florida term"—and found himself living in Missouri...

By now Heather appeared to have lost interest in the flow of words coming—was it from Florida? Or merely from across the white tablecloth?

While Michel continued his memoirs, Anna said in a private aside, "What's the first thing you plan to do in Chicago, Heather?"

"Get a job. Find a place where I can paint."

Michel paused for a swallow of coffee. Anna had seldom seen him when his mouth and jaw weren't moving. He set down his cup. "Do you have any contacts in Chicago, Heather?"

"Not to speak of."

"I know a lot of people in Miami," he said.

"All I need is a Chicago name or two. A studio. A gallery. I'll take it from there."

"No matter what city you're in," Michel said, "beware of galleries. They take too much money."

"You opened your own gallery, didn't you?" said one of the women.

"Yes," he said. "I paid the commissions to myself and myself alone."

"My father used to host a potters' collective in his studio," said Heather.

"No, no, no, no, no," said Michel in a quick succession of opinion. "Collectives have their own set of problems."

"It worked for my father. He cares more about art than money."

Michel raised an eyebrow—"a questionable concept"—and resumed his autobiography. "When I sold my gallery..."

Half listening to the man's ruminations, Anna watched Heather scoot her chair back from the table in an abrupt show of boredom that was either unnoticed or ignored by Michel as he traveled through the Miami of his mind.

Recently Sebastian had shared a rare confidence: His daughter worried him. "She's a little opinionated," he'd said. When asked what he meant, he said she sometimes didn't realize that other people were as real as she was. "Maybe I've given her too much freedom," he said. "Taught her to criticize other people. Been too individualistic. Defied convention."

Well, yes, Anna thought. *You've defied convention.* Certainly Heather's beginnings defied convention. Eighteen-some years earlier, pale and serious, Sebastian had appeared at Anna's doorstep needing to talk, he'd said, because there was going to be a big change in his life. While he went for a beer, she'd backed up to the sofa, a fragment of thought whining like a bullet past her face. *He's found another woman. He doesn't love me anymore.*

She'd been half right. He'd found another woman. But he loved Anna; that wouldn't change, he assured her. He wanted a child, so he'd set about finding a mother. Anna listened, too astonished to comprehend. Wasn't it usually the woman who set about looking for the father? Researching sources for good genes? Getting background information at the sperm bank?

In Sebastian's case, he'd gone looking for superior eggs.

Why not me? Anna inwardly screamed after she'd had time to think. *Why not me as the mother?* But of course she was no longer ovulating.

For a while she refused to sleep with him. He actually began using the telephone to contact her. Seeing his efforts, she was somewhat mollified. His courtship suffered a setback, however, when she asked him who the woman was and he refused to tell her.

"Do you like her?" Anna asked.

"Not particularly," Sebastian said. "We never talk. She'll call when the baby's born."

"Was the sex good?"

"Not particularly, though not unpleasant."

"Not unpleasant!" Anna exclaimed.

"I've had some sexual experience over the past thirty years or so."
Sebastian was forty-nine at the time, Anna, sixty. "Much of it with you—"

"Much of it with me!"

"Most of it with you."

She was unimpressed.

"I've stayed with you, haven't I?"

He had. Still, she kept her Woodland Street door locked until he rang
the doorbell one rainy night. She let him in because he was wet, she was
miserable without him, and she saw that he wasn't really interested in sex
with anyone but her.

"She's gone into labor," he said simply.

Anna was stunned. "Shouldn't you be there?"

"I don't want to be there and she doesn't want me to be there," he
said. "Don't you realize yet that this is a transaction?"

"Are you paying her?"

"Eight thousand dollars," he said, rolling up his black umbrella and
hanging it on the outside doorknob. She opened the door and he came
in, dripping.

He raised Heather so outside a traditional family that schoolteachers,
even social workers, called him in for conferences. Over the years, when
Anna attempted closeness with the girl, she felt father and daughter pull
away in a subtle rebuff. Though she raised her own daughter for a very
short time, she was more than satisfied with those three years. She'd been
a good mother!

In one of Anna's indelible memories, her little daughter turns her
back on the outgrown crib in the corner. *I not a baby,* she declares, shaking her head and flapping the blanket across her new bed. *Big girl now!*
That sense of self, that radiant smile, would be gone within the year. The
child was right: she would never need the crib again. Never the big-girl
bed, either.

"I think we make the choice very early in our lives, possibly in infancy," Michel was declaiming from the other side of the tablecloth.

Anna looked over at his two admirers whose faces told her nothing
except that they adored him.

"I'm sorry," she interrupted. "I missed that. What choice are you
talking about?"

He seemed only too happy to repeat himself. "What if we have
a choice of bandwidth, so to speak—frequency, spectrum, color, at-
titude—for living our lives? And what if that choice is presented at

our first breath?" Warming to his own words, he leaned forward, his well-shaped hands defining the enormity of his theory. "What if, with the first thwack of the midwife—'*Choose! Choose!*'—the first squall of the newborn—'*Not yet! Not yet!*'—we have to make a decision that will determine our characters, our futures, our very destinies?" He sank back against his chair, astounded. "Yet we can't possibly know enough at birth to make this all-important choice that will affect the rest of our lives."

The two women listened, out of their depth. Anna put her elbows on the table and considered the statement before deciding that she, too, was out of her depth. But Heather said with excitement, "I've had some of those same thoughts myself. In fact," she pulled out a smart phone, "I painted something," and she brushed the screen furiously, searching for a particular photograph. "I call it *Choice*. It's about the very thing, the very concept, you're describing." She circumnavigated the table until she was standing beside Michel. Holding the screen in front of his face, she said, "Each colored rod in the row depicts a particular harmony in a piece of music I was listening to."

He seemed baffled. "What is the music?" he finally asked.

"Bach," she exclaimed. "I mapped out the measures and used greens and blues whenever the key returned to A major."

"Hmm," said Michel. "Are you a musician?"

"Not exactly. I've looked into theory and harmony, but I'm first and foremost a visual artist."

"Hmm," said Michel. "It *does* resemble a piano keyboard. And the medium is?"

"Pastels on pastel paper. Dry pigment pressed into a stick with some binder. But in case you don't want to think in terms of music," she added, snapping the phone shut and returning to her place beside Anna, "you could assume that each rod, each bar, each color occupies an existential value."

The two women looked mystified.

"Don't you see? It's pretty much the same thing you're talking about," Heather insisted, "except in the case of my painting, it would be metaphoric."

"I have no objection to music," Michel said, beside the point. A lame silence hung over the table. "I work in copper, myself."

Heather, barely hiding exasperation, remained at the table a few minutes longer before leaving abruptly. Anna pushed back her chair and straggled behind.

"Whether you work in copper or pastels or—egg tempera," Heather stormed under her breath as she and Anna made their way toward the elevators, "it's the concept that matters."

"Choice," Anna said thoughtfully. The elevator arrived and the doors slid apart. "Moral choice."

Heather frowned. "What do you mean, 'moral choice'?"

"Well, whether this hypothetical person, perhaps Michel's fictitious infant, makes the choice to be decent, fair-minded, even-handed, responsible—"

"You're over-simplifying," Heather said dismissively as they reached the fifth floor.

"Each quality is one of your painted rods," Anna continued. "Cheerful or sullen, saintly or criminal, well-integrated or bipolar—"

"You're confusing a lot of issues, Anna." As soon as Heather stepped off the elevator, the apartment door opened and Sebastian stood before them, dressed in slacks, sports jacket, and tie.

"Dad! What are you doing here?"

What she meant, Anna thought, was *what are you doing here in a jacket and tie?*

"I came to talk to you," he said. Inside, Heather dropped onto the sofa and folded her arms sharply. Off-balance and disjointed, Sebastian pivoted from Heather to Anna and back to Heather. "I'd like to go to Chicago with you and stay till you're settled."

"What if I'm not ready to leave yet?"

"I thought you were packed and ready to go!"

Their voices followed Anna down the hall and into the bedroom, rising to the level of argument, teetering back to low-level disagreement. By the time she returned, Heather was gone. Sebastian stood at the window, looking out at the woods.

"She left?" Anna said, noting how the slacks and sports jacket enhanced his height. Even his wiry hair was under control.

He turned around and snapped his fingers. "Just like that." He sat down at one end of the sofa.

Anna joined him and took one of his hands. "Has she delayed her move?"

"She isn't telling me anything," he fumed. "I don't think she knows what she's doing." He fell into a distracted silence.

"You look good in disguise," Anna said, gently touching the knot of his necktie, the hem of his sports jacket.

"What do you think?" he finally said.

"About what?"

"About Heather. Do you think she's ready to make this move?" He almost never asked her opinion, especially about his daughter.

"She's eighteen."

"But is she ready?" There was controlled desperation in his voice. Was he dressing conventionally today because he thought he could convey a last-minute message of common sense to Heather? Of ordinary, mainstream behavior? Or was he just now realizing how much he would miss her? "My daughter and I have lived without a lot of rules," he admitted.

"True."

"Is it too late to start now?"

"Probably."

It had taken Anna until Heather's tenth birthday to stop wanting a conventional family. She never confused Heather with Marianna. She didn't want Heather for her own daughter. She simply wanted a family.

Ultimately, instead of gaining a family, she gained clarity. Sebastian and Heather were their own family. The girl had operated without a mother since infancy and she didn't need one now. With time, Anna realized what she herself needed was enough love and intimacy to feel complete. Enough fuel to do her work. And Sebastian, a younger man whom she loved.

"You've always liked rules more than I do," Sebastian said grudgingly.

"In the past, yes," she agreed. "But I don't need them now."

He flared, reversing himself. "That's because you don't have to worry about a child."

She struggled to her feet in an eruption that surprised both of them. *"I would give anything to worry about my child!"* Sebastian tried and failed to pull her down beside him. When she finally dropped onto the cushions, he put his arms around her and pressed his cheek to the tears running down her face. Sebastian's face was hot with alarm. After a few shuddering breaths, she fell silent.

"I'm sorry, Anna! I didn't realize!" He stroked her hair, tended to her like a child, blamed himself. "I wanted to be a father," he finally said.

"You *are* a father, Sebastian."

He leaned back into the sofa. "I haven't told you everything."

Anna sat quietly, drained.

"Heather's been in touch with someone on the internet."

Silence.

"In Chicago." Like an underwater swimmer punching through the surface, he flung back his head, spraying self-revelation. "I've never set rules for her use of the computer, or much of anything else. I thought she had a right to privacy and I never interfered or even asked what she was doing." He lowered his head, confused. "But now I wonder if she had too much freedom."

No reaction.

"A few weeks ago I heard her side of a conversation. She was asking about a gallery—in Chicago, I found out later. What she was saying worried me."

A stirring of interest.

"This person was promising her an entire exhibit in a gallery. She was very excited. 'I can fill the walls,' I heard her say. 'I have a lot of completed work.' The talk seemed to turn personal. She was flirting with someone on the other end of her earphones. She sounded clumsy." He paused. "It dawned on me that she's never had a boyfriend." He stood and returned to the window. "I found the guy."

So this is why you stayed away longer than you wanted to.

"How did you find him?" she asked, sidestepping the obvious question: *Who is he?*

Sebastian picked up a magazine from the end table. "I hired a detective."

"Who is the man?"

But that was all he would say.

What a delicate mechanism of privacy and defense he possesses, she thought on her way to the kitchen. At the sink, pressing a wet cloth to her face, she recognized that she, too, probably had mechanisms for self-protection, though she didn't know what they were. She leaned against the counter, very tired. She would have to wait, she knew, to learn more about the man on the internet; that is, if Sebastian ever mentioned him again.

"Heather has always seemed very sure of herself," she said, returning to the living room.

"I thought so, too. Now I question whether I've ever really known my daughter."

Chapter Eight

"Have you heard?" said Meg, wide-eyed. She'd made a special trip to Anna's apartment on the way down to breakfast. "It's about your nephew."

Anna's heart contracted. Even as she waited, the thought struck like a bird against window glass: *bad news before breakfast.*

"It's Nahum," said Philip, coming up behind his wife. "They let the colored boy go."

"Philip!" his wife scolded. Anna turned her back on the neighbors. She needed to sit.

"I'm sorry we blundered in like this," said Meg excitedly, following her inside. "Nahum has lost his job!" Anna let herself down into the rocking chair and gestured weakly toward the sofa while Philip hovered in the hallway.

"Could you let in some air?" Anna said. If she could feel a fresh breeze move through the apartment, she might be able to hear what Meg so badly wanted to tell her. She would listen, then ask the woman to leave.

"It's a nice sunny morning," Meg said mindlessly, returning from opening the sliding glass door in the bedroom. They heard the elevator doors close behind Philip.

Fresh air did not help after all. A strong wind might. A gale.

"What happened to Nahum?" Anna asked almost inaudibly.

"I hate to say it, but he's been fired."

Anna tried to say "why?" but no sound came.

"I'm not sure why," Meg said. *Perhaps she had actually said the word?*

The woman perched on the edge of a sofa cushion. "Something about a connection to—a house of ill repute."

"Nahum?"

"That's what they're saying."

"Where did you hear this crude rumor?" Anna snapped.

"The neighbor on the other side of us."

"Well, well, well," she said, beginning to rock.

Grasping the arm-rest of the sofa, Meg scooted her rangy, sinewy body impossibly forward. "Can I get you anything? A glass of water? Would you like to come down and eat with us, or at least have a cup of coffee?"

Anna could think of nothing she would rather not do. "No, I'll sit here and wait until Nahum comes and talks to me."

"He may already be gone," Meg warned. "Someone said his office has been cleared out."

"He'll come." Something in Anna's face motivated her neighbor to stand and walk to the door.

"You're sure you want to stay here alone?" said Meg just before stepping into the hallway.

She probably meant *stay here alone for the moment*, but to Anna it carried an ominous meaning: *Are you sure you want to stay here alone at The Oaks without Nahum?*

He arrived an hour later, breaking through Anna's dazed thoughts.

She lifted her arms and he knelt in front of the rocking chair, encircling her waist, resting against her, almost as if he were a child again. Pulling away, he positioned a straight chair beside her and took her hand.

"What am I hearing?" Anna said after a silence in which she placed her free hand on top of his. He wasn't able to speak and so she bided her time, their hands resting on her knee, the rocking chair creaking rhythmically.

"My neighbor stopped by this morning," Anna finally said. "I don't believe her."

Nahum slowly moved his head from side to side, his own form of rocking. Standing, he went to the sofa and rubbed his eyes and wet cheeks with the heels of his hands. How Anna had loved the hands of her husband, Nahum's uncle: the fingertips, palms light in color, sweet receptors for her touch. "It's my brother-in-law."

Anna could not place the man.

"My wife's brother," Nahum added. "Vicki's brother."

"Have I met him?"

"I doubt it." He stood again, put his hands in the pockets of his Levi's, and began to pace methodically around the room. Pausing in front of Sebastian's teapot, he touched its handle. As if the pottery provided strength—dirt, clay, water—he said, "It's Tim." He stopped, sat down, stood up, resumed his pacing. "He's up to his neck in trouble and he's dragging the rest of us down with him."

In his agonized travel he stepped behind the rocking chair, moving from sofa to wall and back to the sofa. Anna listened carefully, hearing his steps and voice behind her, seeing his face when he emerged into view, losing his expression as he paced behind her again. Once more he dropped onto the sofa. "Tim took a minor into his house and locked her up. He's charged with trafficking. Charged with a felony."

Anna repositioned herself, her arms on the armrests, her body almost pitching forward. She looked like what she was: an old woman in danger of falling from a rocking chair onto the floor.

"I heard the term 'house of ill repute' this morning," she said.

"Tim's house," Nahum said. "His brothel. His whore house."

She pushed herself deep into the rocking chair. "What does this have to do with you, Nahum?"

"Family," he said dully.

Anna waited.

"He drove the girl to our house. Someone saw him park in the driveway and take her inside." He gave a muted cry. "The police arrested us!"

"Have you been in jail?" Anna asked, wide-eyed.

"Friends bailed us out. We have to go before a judge."

"And The Oaks has actually fired you?"

"Suspended. That's what they're calling it." Impulsively he stood. "The girl went missing from foster care..." He jammed his hands into his pockets. "Brave, wasn't he, to expose his sister to a criminal charge. I can't talk about it anymore. I came to tell you in person. That's all."

"I can't bear it," Anna said, and did nothing to follow up the statement except to touch his hand as he left the apartment. Neither of them said good-bye.

She went into the bedroom, made her bed, took a sweater from her closet—the dining room downstairs was always chilly—then put it away again. No dining room today. She would have to pass Nahum's office every time she went for meals. Whenever she picked up her mail, his door would be closed. When it opened again, there would be a stranger behind his desk.

In the kitchen she made coffee, poured herself a cup, set the pot on the trivet. But instead of adding cream, she went to the bookcase in the living room and pulled down the textbook she'd written. Though she no longer remembered specific provisions of the law, she knew trafficking was different from prostitution. Trafficking was slavery.

Chapter Nine

"Heather's found a gallery and a studio," Sebastian said on the night of his return from Chicago. "It's both. They call it a resident arts building." Since he didn't like to talk on the telephone, Anna had to wait for an account until he was home again.

Account wasn't the right word. Sebastian didn't like to account for himself. Once, when she pressed him too hard for an accounting, he stayed away for weeks. Finally, not to apologize, not to say either of them was wrong, she went to his studio and slid a note under his door: "I miss you. Anna."

And he came back.

She would have loved to receive a phone call from Heather in Chicago. *Anna, I'm crazy about Chicago! I've found the perfect place, not just a gallery or a studio* ... But Heather would not call to share her excitement. To Heather, Anna was unimportant; simply her father's girlfriend.

"She can work and exhibit in the arts building," Sebastian was saying, "and live in a house with several young artists like herself."

"How far is the house from the studio?" Anna asked, practical.

"A ten-minute walk." Leaning back on pillows piled against the headboard, an open book upside-down on his chest, he turned with a surprised look on his face. "She's making a life in Chicago and she's doing it by herself."

"And the fellow on the internet?" she couldn't help asking.

Sebastian shrugged. "Apparently a thing of the past."

In the darkness outside, a breeze came up and moved through the thick stand of oaks beyond the balcony. Watching the restless, almost audible shadows, he added, "Of course, she still has some growing up to do. She's only eighteen."

Anna brushed her hand through his hair. "She'll learn all she needs to learn..." She cut short the platitude when he took her hand. She'd been waiting for this: his tender attention arriving of its own accord, not because she willed it, but because he had the delicious gift of waiting. If he wasn't ready, then he didn't take her hand; didn't give her a long, intimate kiss; didn't slip his hands under her nightgown; *did* restrain her caresses. If she, too, waited, didn't hurry him, slowly let herself slip into the erotic stream, gently moved against him, sought his accumulating power, they would begin to ride a wave that carried them forward until, floating, lifting, falling, they finally released each other into sleep.

In earlier years, sex had been a shallow container for bright splashing. Sensation. Now it was a vessel, like Sebastian's pottery, breakable, expressive, formed by love and years of history together.

She'd needed Sebastian's sexual love more than she needed to talk about Nahum. But the next morning, lying against him, her voice rough from disuse, she said, "Nahum's been fired."

He reached for her hand. Squinting in the daylight, moving his head higher on the pillow in order to see her, he slowly examined her face. "Why?"

Her face, she knew, was wrecked. Between the time Nahum lost his job and last night's restorative lovemaking, she'd hardly slept. "It's his wife's brother. His name is Tim and he runs a brothel out of his house." She explained that the police knew about it, Nahum knew about it, the neighbors who lived near Tim on their half-acre lots knew about it.

Sebastian threw off the blankets and sat up. "You can be sure plenty of others know about it, too, Anna."

Absentmindedly smoothing the edge of the pillowcase, she said, "Do you know about it, Sebastian?"

He stood, picked up his underwear, and walked to the straight chair where he'd left his shirt and pants. "No. But places like that have always existed and there are always people who know about them."

"Yes, of course," said Anna, sitting up against the headboard. "But this girl is a minor. And she was locked inside the brother-in-law's house, along with other women."

Sebastian frowned and shook out his clothes.

"It's more than prostitution," Anna said. "It's trafficking."

"How is Nahum involved?"

"This Tim called his sister and said the police were on the way. He just took the minor and ran."

"Where?"

"To Nahum's house."

He transferred his clothes from one arm to the other. "Who called the police?"

"I don't know," Anna said, raising her voice.

"Where was Nahum?"

Anna leaned forward and braced herself. "He wasn't even at home when it happened. He found his brother-in-law handcuffed and Vicki against the wall being questioned." She dropped back against the headboard. "For Heaven's sake, Sebastian, don't you believe him? Don't you believe *me*?"

"I've been out of town, Anna. This is the first I've heard about it."

"If you would use the telephone once in a while..."

He carried his clothes into the bathroom. Above the sounds of running water, Anna considered him in first one light, then another. Over their forty years together, they'd spent time apart, but she never had reason to worry about unfaithfulness. Except for the brief liaison with Heather's mother—and that was because he wanted a child.

"Where is Tim now?" Sebastian said, emerging from the bathroom in Levi's and work shirt.

She slowly shook her head. "I don't know."

"You haven't talked to Nahum?"

"He has a lot on his mind."

"Call him," said Sebastian.

"He'll contact me when he's ready," she said.

Sebastian carried his shoes and socks to the chair by the window. When he finished with the laces, he straightened. "I've forgotten Nahum's last name."

She turned her head sharply against the headboard.

"I've been gone, Anna. I want to know what happened."

"Orland," she said. "He's my nephew. My husband's brother's son."

Sebastian made a gesture of forgetfulness. "Of course." Still seated, he leaned his forearms on his knees and clasped his hands loosely. "You're waiting for Nahum to call you? Maybe he can't." He stepped across the room and sat on the edge of the bed close to her. "Is he in jail?"

"He didn't do anything!" She thought of her husband's false arrest during a late-night walk. *"It's not safe for a Black man to forget he's Black," Lorenzo had said.*

You and I cannot grasp the injustice, she thought. Pushing herself to a sitting position, she said again, "He'll call when he's ready."

"It isn't like you not to call, Anna." Sebastian rested his hand on her wrist and concentrated. "Your pulse is jumping. It's uneven."

"I'm upset."

Sebastian studied her, crossed to the dresser, and picked up the keys to his truck. "You might feel better if you talk to him."

Hearing the front door open and close, Anna slid back down in bed and stared at the sliding glass door and the woods beyond. Nahum's assumed guilt was like the name *Orland* on a label showing above a dirty collar, bringing down the entire Black-and-White family. Sebastian couldn't really understand. His sympathy was limited by what he'd experienced—no, by what he *hadn't* experienced.

Chapter Ten

Hovering at the edge of the dining room, Anna spotted a turquoise blouse with Georgina inside it, gesticulating from a center table. The woman smiled broadly as Anna approached. Flicking a white linen napkin across her bright yardage, she exclaimed, "Join us! I've missed you in the 'hood."

"I've missed you, too, Georgina."

Orville, her husband, leaned forward and spoke around his wife. "Georgina was just saying she hasn't seen you in the dining room recently."

"I've been eating in my apartment the last few days," said Anna, seating herself next to Georgina.

"Welcome back," he continued. "I offered to go up and find you, but Georgina here says, 'No, she'll be down in her own good time.' 'She must be hibernating,' I says. 'She'll be down now that it's spring.'" He smiled and leaned back, ready to eat.

"The salmon sounds good," said Georgina.

"And berries for dessert," said Anna. "Just right for a bear coming out of hibernation."

At the table behind them, Michel was soliloquizing. "The art world in Miami was particularly profitable when my wife and I moved down from New York and opened a gallery."

Georgina leaned toward Anna. "The man is tireless."

Bringing his reminiscences to a temporary close, Michel dabbed at his mouth with a corner of white linen and rose from the table. The women in the room focused on his silver hair and smart tailoring as he brushed past them, pausing at Anna's table. "We must share a meal one of these days," he said to all three, "along with Sebastian and his daughter."

"Let's do that," Georgina replied cheerfully.

"Has Heather found her way to Chicago yet?" Michel asked.

"I believe she has," said Anna.

"It's a tough world, art," he said. "Selling your own work is the only way to go." He continued his promenade out of the dining room.

Orville speared a cherry tomato from the salad. "Have we met Sebastian?"

"Anna's boyfriend," Georgina explained.

"Not a husband who's always underfoot?"

Georgina smiled and patted his arm indulgently. "People warned me about retired husbands underfoot all day," she said to Anna. "'He'll mope around the house with nothing to do,' everyone warned me, so I made a list of things that needed to be done and titled it *Orville.*"

"Honey-do's," said Orville.

"I used to love to-do lists," Anna said. "When I was still on Woodland Street I had a little blackboard in the kitchen with an eraser that I cleaned once a week by hitting it against a fence post in the backyard."

"What things were on your list?" asked Georgina. Orville, too, looked interested.

"Oh, *Water plants,*" said Anna. "*Clean the bathroom. Finish Chapter 10.*"

"Georgina never had a blackboard," said Orville. "Her memory is like a Jaws of Life."

"What's a Jaws of Life?" asked Georgina.

"A steel instrument that can cut through any material made by God or man."

"It also saves lives," said Anna.

"Well, that, too."

"Very little escapes my attention," Georgina said, gripping her fork.

"How many chapters are in your book?" Orville asked.

"Twenty-two."

"I can't imagine writing even one," said Georgina. "How do you start?"

"By telling the readers what I'm going to tell them," said Anna. "Then in the middle I tell them what I'm telling them, and at the end I tell them what I've told them."

"How do you know when you're at the end?"

"Simple," said Anna. "I can't think of anything more to say." As if the same principle applied to conversation, they stopped talking and finished their salads. A new resident came through the door of the dining room, a quiet man with soft steps, an understated man who stung Anna with his presence, a reminder that Nahum would no longer enter the room to swing her hands in his, chat in a musical voice, invite her for coffee.

Georgina re-flicked her napkin.

"How do you spend your time here at The Oaks, Georgina?" Anna said.

"Well, of course I keep the apartment picked up—"

"My socks," said Orville.

"—and make the bed."

Orville looked hurt.

"Actually, we make the bed together," Georgina admitted.

"Only fair since we unmake it together," Orville said naughtily.

Georgina snorted. "Monday, arts and crafts. Tuesday, flower arrangements for the lobby. Wednesday, Cooking For Fun With Gladys—"

"Don't forget the swim team," said Orville.

"Swim team?" said Anna.

"There are several," Georgina said. "We're The Sharks." She pushed her plate back.

"Originally they were The Walruses," said Orville.

"Then we started working with a trainer and he thought we should change our name," said Georgina. "I can't remember what they're having for dessert today. Did you notice?"

"Mixed berry cobbler," said Orville.

Anna, too, pushed back her plate. "What time do The Sharks swim?"

"Nine o'clock on the dot. I can stop by for you tomorrow morning. Bring your bathing suit."

Anna hung from the edge of the pool, her arms draped along the tiles, slowly moving her legs underwater. Watching The Sharks in their aquatic exercise circle, listening to the commands of the leader, proved to be enough for the first day. It had been months since she'd exercised, either above or below water. Paddling toward an unoccupied lane, she slipped under the shimmering surface, heard the muffled calls in the world above before emerging from the watery world below. Rolling onto her back, she propelled herself in a straight line by following an overhead beam painted red. Her bathing suit still fit, though the short skirt brushed annoyingly against her thighs, as if she were swimming through tall grass. But how good, after eighty years, to have a body at all. To move freely, ageless and weightless. For a moment she relinquished herself to the water and floated. Regret and anxiety exchanged their grip for tender, cradling arms, and she lay, resting, on the surface of the water.

Later, feeling as if her skin had been sloughed off and replaced by a fresh, new layer, she walked with Georgina toward the double doors separating the pool from the public rooms.

"We'll have to get you a locker," Georgina said, glancing at the bag swinging by Anna's side. "You can keep your stuff in the dressing room." In spite of a shower and shampoo, Anna could still smell chlorine in her hair. In the water, she'd entered a world that held no trace of the worries that so often cycled through her mind. Now, however, merely passing by the closed door to Nahum's old office snatched away the freedom she'd felt in the water.

"I miss Nahum," she confided.

"I miss him, too," said Georgina, dropping into the first chair they came to. "Let's sit," she declared, as if she hadn't already. Almost shaking an imaginary cane at the walls, she said vehemently, "There is no reason for Nahum not to be here at The Oaks."

"There's a reason but not a *good* reason," said Anna, taking the chair opposite.

"Do you think he'd still be here if he was White?" Like a fast-leaking balloon, Georgina's question swooped and whistled through the lobby before it settled, shrunken, at Anna's feet.

"Yes, I think he would still be here if he were White," she said.

"I remember when he was hired," Georgina said. "They didn't used to have a deputy director, you know. They added the position when The Oaks expanded."

Anna did not know that.

"Oh, yes," said Georgina. "A number of residents complained when he was hired." She glanced into the middle distance and back again. "You know, Anna, a lot of people are prejudiced."

Anna almost smiled.

"But," Georgina added, "he'd still be here if it wasn't for his brother's sex crime."

"Brother-in-law," Anna corrected.

"Have you called Nahum?" Georgina asked.

"No," she answered. "I haven't talked to him."

"Well, for heaven's sake, give him a call," said Georgina.

Anna's face passed slowly from passive to active, like a soufflé achieving firmness. She got to her feet and started down the hallway.

"I'll come with you as far as the café," Georgina called out. Michel emerged from the library as first Anna, then Georgina, filed past. Startled, keeping to the wall out of range of the swinging bag, he explained unnecessarily, "I've just been reading the morning papers."

"You mean bad news from one newspaper isn't enough?" said Georgina.

"You have to read beyond the headlines," said Michel. The remark surprised Anna who paused at the entrance to the café.

"Your nephew's termination is shameful," he said when he caught up to her. Uncertain about this new, serious Michel, Anna's focus moved from the café door to the lapel of his sports jacket. "The man has two strikes against him," he opined further. "First, his name is publicly connected with a criminal matter, and"— he put up a second finger—"he's Black." He slowly shook his classically shaped head. "Either one might have been enough to remove him, but taken together, he didn't have a chance."

"Let's have coffee," Anna said impulsively, stepping into the cafe. "Put everything on my tab," she told the in-house cashier with such authority that Georgina and Michel obediently walked to the coffee urn in the corner and began filling their cups. When they'd all slid into the booth under the wall clock shaped like a frying pan, she said, "I've been spending too much time alone."

"That, and you need to talk to Nahum," Georgina said.

Anna cocked her head. "I've tried to avoid the whole thing. I've even stopped following the news."

"According to the newspaper," said Michel, "Nahum has testified in court."

Georgina raised an eyebrow. "They've already had the trial?"

"The police arrested the brother—" he continued.

"Brother-in-law," said Anna.

"—in Nahum's house but they exceeded their authority when they arrested Nahum."

"How come this went to trial so fast?" said Georgina. "Nothing ever goes to trial this fast."

"Preliminary hearing," Anna said. "Probable cause."

"They have to show it's a solid case against the brother-in-law, is that it?" said Georgina.

"According to the newspaper, they've done that," said Michel.

"Can we call him the defendant?" said Anna. "*Brother-in-law* sounds..."

"I'm sorry," said Georgina. She looked kindly at Anna. "It's not Nahum's fault his relative is a criminal."

"He's not a blood relative," said Michel.

"They still have to prove the crime," Anna reminded her.

Eyes alight, Georgina refused to be bullied. "You mean innocent until proven guilty?" She waved her hand. "How can anyone mistreat a young girl the way Nahum's—the way this defendant has done and be innocent?"

Georgina's understanding of the legal system hung heavily over the table. "You're unusually quiet," she said, turning to Michel.

"Am I usually talking?"

"Yes," said Georgina.

"Camouflage," he said.

Anna centered her cup in its saucer. "I'd rather see Nahum face-to-face than talk to him on the telephone, but he probably won't want to come to The Oaks."

"He could visit you in the evening after the dining room and lobby have cleared out," said Georgina. "He wouldn't have to see anyone."

"He'd be uncomfortable here," said Anna.

"If Orville and I still had our car, we could drive you," said Georgina. "But we're not safe behind the wheel anymore."

"If I still drove," said Michel, "I'd take you wherever you wanted to go."

"What kind of a car did you have?" asked Georgina.

"Mercedes. When I couldn't pass the driving test without glasses, I sold it."

"I've never seen you wear glasses," Georgina said.

"That's because I never do."

Georgina smiled. "Vanity." Michel didn't dispute it. "But surely," she continued, "you could give up a little vanity in order to get a driver's license."

Michel leaned his head back against the booth. "Without my wife, going places isn't fun anymore."

"I'm sorry," Georgina said.

"It must be difficult," Anna added. Neither woman had considered that Michel might be lonely.

He rattled a sugar packet and tore off one corner. "As a lawyer," he said, turning to Anna, "you probably know something about trafficking."

"Not much," said Anna. "There's a big difference between being a professor of law and a practicing attorney."

"Do you talk about specific trafficking cases in your book?"

She didn't remember ever telling him about her book. "Well, yes, there are summaries of several cases."

"Anything comparable to Nahum's situation?"

"Nahum wasn't involved," Georgina reminded him.

"True," said Michel, "but do you know of any cases where there was a conspiracy, you might call it?"

"Oh, like a kidnapping ring?" said Georgina.

"I'm thinking hypothetically," said Michel.

Unable to think hypothetically about Nahum, Anna looked at the clock on the wall and began gathering up her swim bag. "I've already waited too long to call," she said.

Michel withdrew a folded sheet of paper from the inner pocket of his jacket.

"What have you got there?" Georgina asked.

"A letter to The Oaks corporate office."

"Can you read it to us?"

"Not without glasses," said Michel.

"Well, how do you ever read anything at all?"

"I don't. That's why I talk so much." Nevertheless, squinting, he began. "Dear Ms. Whitman, as a resident of The Oaks Retirement Center in Huntridge, Missouri, I wish to express my dismay at the recent termination of Nahum Orland, Deputy Director."

"Oh, that's good," said Georgina.

Anna, looking pale, got to her feet. "I need to go upstairs."

"Of course, I won't send it until the wording is right," he said loudly enough for Anna to hear as she departed.

"Of course," said Georgina. But once the letter was back in his inner pocket, she lost interest. Following Anna's example, she left the cafe.

Michel wandered into the lobby, where Anna found him a half hour later.

"Have you seen Georgina?" she asked.

"She left," Michel said. "We adjourned the meeting. Without the chairperson, we had no agenda."

Outside, under the building's overhang, The Oaks van was picking up residents for the weekly trip to the library.

"You're not going to the library?"

"Not today," Anna said. "I'm waiting for Nahum." Her face betrayed quiet triumph. She felt better. Her pulse was calm. The telephone conversation had yielded an unexpected result: Nahum was coming to pick her up. She took a chair by the entrance. With undisguised joy she began babbling to Michel, who hovered nearby. "We're going out for lunch in broad daylight, which means he isn't hiding, creeping about town after hours as if he has to camouflage himself in darkest night.

The charges against him have been dropped and he has a job interview next week—"

"May I join you for a moment?" Michel said, preparing to sit across from her. Even in the midst of unburdening, Anna noticed his courtesy.

"We're going to The Country Diner just outside of town," she continued, looking around the room. "It will be wonderful to get away from The Oaks."

"Nahum is a resilient fellow," Michel said as they watched the van pull away from the curb.

"He's angry, though," she said.

"He has a lot to be angry about."

"I've seen such cruelty toward Blacks," Anna said. "Whites can be an abomination."

Nahum's car rolled up to the entrance. Looking confident, his unbuttoned sports jacket swaying easily, the close haircut shaped to his forehead and jaw, he came around and hugged his aunt before settling her in the passenger seat. Stepping back behind the wheel, he drove off with a short squeal of tires, the only show of contempt for his former place of employment.

Chapter Eleven

They passed the converted warehouse where Sebastian lived and worked. She used to drive there in her little Cooper, drop in on him, have a cup of tea, watch him work if he was at the wheel. Never stay too long. They both had lives. Now she hadn't seen the warehouse since before her accident. A mile farther on, below the limestone brow of the hospital looming above the old railroad trestle, she thought of her husband's suicide; of the emergency team rounding the corner, crepe soles squealing, a sudden stop beside a hospital bed...

Nahum took his eyes off the road long enough to smile at her. With that, the hospital images receded and she began to notice the pleasant forward motion of the car picking up speed as they passed the city limits. The earth smelled damp from last night's rain and the sky was a tender blue. And look! A school yard. Children swinging, higher and higher until, as if in a playground from her childhood, she could hear ropes creaking in their arcs. After a few minutes more of driving, Nahum parked in The Country Diner's asphalt lot overlooking a pasture where cattle grazed.

Her inlaws had always come here after baptisms and funerals. In no hurry to leave the car, she and Nahum reminisced about the summers he stayed behind while his parents were in Dallas for medical treatment. Another hospital...

"How have you been, Aunt Anna?" Nahum asked, turning to face her, resting his back against the driver's door.

"The question, Nahum, is how are you?"

He gazed out the windshield as if distant, forest-covered hills hiding fields and crops in their folds would help him answer. "We're okay. We'd be better if Vicki's brother worked for a living instead of taking criminal shortcuts." A vein throbbed in his temple.

"I guess he's been outside the law for a while," Anna said.

Nahum chuckled without pleasure. "He's played with fire his entire life." A woman came out of the diner's back door, shook several dish-towels, and hung them on a clothesline. "Over the years I've distanced myself from him."

"I never met him," Anna said.

"Vicki tries to shield him." He shook his head. "Her little brother."

"Is this the first time he's locked a woman in the house?"

"I doubt it," Nahum said, "but this time it made the news."

"I can hardly grasp what he's done." Anna traced the lettering on the glove compartment. "I'm sorry I didn't call you sooner."

"You did call."

"Too late, though. I felt sick over your termination."

He groaned involuntarily. "You work so hard to lift up the family. And then a rotten relative brings you down." He'd started sweating and took a handkerchief from his pocket.

"I'm thinking of leaving The Oaks," Anna said.

He gave her a sharp glance before refolding the handkerchief. "That might be premature."

"It makes me heart-sore to see your old office," she said. "Every time I walk past it—"

"Wait," he said. "Knowing you're in a good retirement home gives me peace of mind."

"Good retirement home?"

"The Oaks is well run, Aunt Anna." He was trying to be fair, she knew, but the vein in his temple was throbbing again. "They've screwed up, but remember, originally they treated me right."

Anna looked puzzled.

"They hired me."

"And why wouldn't they? Let's not give them undeserved credit." She put her hand on his forearm. "You're missed. Everyone knows you should still be there. Even Michel—"

"Hah!"

"Even Michel knows you belong at The Oaks."

"How *is* the world-famous artist?"

"Recently he's been bringing up topics unrelated to Florida and his gallery. You, for example."

"What does he say?"

"Assumed guilt by association.

"Assumed guilt by being Black." When he opened the door, a fresh gust replenished the used air in the automobile. They crossed the asphalt and stepped onto grass studded with dandelions.

"I can't believe I'm hungry," Anna said as they entered the diner and read the daily special from a blackboard above the counter: meatloaf and mashed potatoes.

"It's our bodies reminding us…"

Anna looked up at him expectantly.

"Of something." He shrugged. "Don't ask me what."

"Michel has been following the case," Anna said as they chose a table in the corner. "I'm afraid I've hidden from the unpleasantness."

"It sounds like he's branching out into the present," said Nahum, holding a chair for his aunt. Gently he added, "*You're* not retreating, are you, Aunt Anna?"

"Perhaps I am," she said thoughtfully. "Sebastian thinks I am. He wanted me to call you immediately."

Nahum picked up his water glass and set it back down again. "Sebastian isn't exactly the man to criticize you for retreating."

Anna smiled.

"Do you know where he is now?"

"No." After a moment she added, "He has a lot on his mind."

"Oh? What?"

Anna shrugged. "I'm never sure. He questions the world."

Nahum half smiled back. "It's a luxury," he said. "You need free time to do that."

"He's arranged his life so he *has* free time." The waitress came for their order. "And he questions himself, you know," she resumed. "He's skeptical about others, but he's skeptical about himself, too." She removed a pill from her pill box. "He's worried about his daughter."

"Hasn't she moved to Chicago?"

"Yes, and she isn't calling him as often as he'd like. Since I haven't heard from him lately, I'm guessing he's driven to Chicago to check up on her. He hates when people check up on *him*, but with Heather it's a different matter." She closed the pill box with a snap. "Before she left, she was talking to a man on the internet."

"The internet," Nahum said without inflection.

"I use e-mail, but as far as the bad sites…"

"There are lots of those," said Nahum, peering over his glasses and studying her above the frames.

Gazing out between flimsy café curtains hanging from brass rings, she said, "I think what worries Sebastian is that Heather has a certain ignorance about people."

"She's been raised alone by Sebastian, hasn't she?"

"Yes. Between that and her internet life—well, she's a talented young woman, but she doesn't realize how little she knows."

He leaned back. "Vicki's brother is the same way. He's ignorant." His eyes narrowed. "And he has contempt for others."

"I think Heather does, too."

"Does Sebastian realize it?"

"No, I don't think he does. He's uneasy about her, though."

"It's hard to recognize your child's personality for what it is," said Nahum. "Or a favorite little brother's."

"Maybe that's what Sebastian is doing in Chicago right now," Anna said. "Realizing how much his daughter doesn't know." She sat in a speculative silence. "I wonder how we learn what we learn."

"Exposure," said Nahum.

"I thought coming to The Oaks meant the end of everything," said Anna. "And now I'm learning more than I wanted to."

Nahum flicked at an imaginary spot on the Formica tabletop. "I'll tell you something I learned and how I learned it." There was such a long pause that it seemed he wasn't going to tell her after all. "It's how I understand my brother-in-law's crime. It's why I despise him."

Anna laid her hand over the sudden pounding in her chest.

"When I was a boy, a teacher raped me." Removing his glasses and setting them on the table, he continued with studious deliberation. "He was adult and White. I was young and Black. It was racial bullying. He knew he could get away with it."

Anna folded her arms tightly against herself.

"He did it because he could. He knew no one would stop him." He paused. "And that's how I know what the girl in Tim's house went through."

Anna twisted her water glass in place. "How old were you?"

"Thirteen."

"I never heard about it," said Anna. "Did you tell anyone?"

"Hardly anyone. Too hard to describe." He thrust his head forward. "I despise my brother-in-law."

"Did he rape the girl?"

Nahum slowly shook his head. "I don't know. He might as well have."

"What about the buyers?"

"What about them?"

"Haven't they been caught?"

"The law doesn't bother much with johns."

"Your parents had grounds for a lawsuit," said Anna after a bit. "You still do."

While her mind registered the shallow legalism, she began to feel a cramping sensation, almost as if dirty water were being pumped into her lower bowel. Her body seemed to register the sexual assaults she'd never been aware of: the girl locked in Tim's house, yes, but the boy Nahum, too. Surely someone would have mentioned it over the years? And why was she oblivious to Tim's brothel? Was it because she was White and Nahum and Vicki had closed Black ranks? Did they not want to shock her? Did they think of her as a schoolgirl? *Was* she still a schoolgirl? The filthy, grainy liquid was traveling urgently now, as if washing up into her stomach, invading her chest and esophagus.

How little she knew.

She sank back in the chair and grabbed at breaths flying by. Folding her numb hands, she thought to herself, *I am going to have a heart attack,* and was surprised when she didn't. Nahum didn't notice her distress, pre-occupied, as he was, with his own. His nervous hands flitted from fork to napkin to tabletop before retreating heavily under the table.

"Can we skip lunch?" he asked, looking at the meatloaf and congealing gravy the waitress had delivered to the table.

Anna nodded and folded her napkin.

"I can't tell Vicki how much I hate her brother," he said as he stood and anchored bills under the salt and pepper shakers. With their untouched food behind them, they walked to the car, shoulders hunched, heads lowered miserably, eyes to the ground. "We can barely talk about his crime, much less about Tim himself." They got in the car. In a heavy silence he drove back to town and parked in a guest spot at The Oaks. Anna stumbled out of the car.

"I'll walk you up to your apartment," he said. She registered surprise. "You don't think I'm afraid to show my face here, do you?"

Once in her apartment, they went directly to the kitchen where Anna filled the chamber of the coffeepot with water. Turning from the sink, she said in a low voice, "I should have noticed you were upset."

He looked puzzled.

"When you were assaulted as a boy."

"It was a long time ago." Expressionless, he watched the thin stream of coffee begin flowing into the pot.

"Did the teacher attack you at school?" she asked after a silence.

"In the coatroom after everyone else had gone." The coffeemaker belched and grew quiet. "He asked me to stay late and help him with something special."

"How did the girl end up in Tim's house?" Anna asked.

"She was about to age out of the foster care system. Tim learned about her. Someone informs someone who informs someone else, who informs—"

"God, Nahum."

"It's ugly," he said. "She's been passed through five different families since she was a child."

Anna stood and poured the coffee. Her hands shook.

"I'll be able to talk to Vicki about her brother when it all blows over," he said unconvincingly.

"Will it ever blow over?" Anna said.

"No."

She went to the refrigerator for cream. "Did Vicki ever go to Tim's house?"

"I think she was careful not to. He always visited *us.*" Nahum pushed his chair back from the table. "I don't like thinking about Tim, much less talking about him. I understand why Vicki avoids the topic."

"Sebastian's heart is in the right place," Anna said, as if they'd been talking about Sebastian's heart, "but he's like Vicki. He keeps things to himself."

Nahum smiled bitterly. "Vicki's hiding from pain."

"I know he was concerned about your termination," she continued, sitting down again at the table. "He actually talked about it. Now it's Heather he's upset about, but he's not talking." In Nahum's silence she heard his thoughts: *hasn't it always been so?* "His habits bother me more than they used to," she admitted.

Nahum studied her. "Does Sebastian like coming to The Oaks?"

"I doubt it, though he understands I can't take care of a big house anymore."

"He liked that house," said Nahum. "So did I. It was a second home to me."

Anna fought a wave of homesickness for 915 Woodland Street. How instantly the automobile accident changed her life. How emotionally reliant she was on Sebastian and now Nahum. How suddenly the awareness of depravity was infiltrating her world. How had she not known about Nahum's childhood rape? What other wickedness was she ignorant of?

She struggled up from self-criticism. "I'm tired of thinking about sexual crime."

"That makes two of us," said Nahum.

"What can I do to make things easier for you?" Anna said.

"Stay at The Oaks for now."

"I won't move without discussing it first," she promised.

&

That evening Anna, Georgina, Orville, and Michel found themselves seated in a corner of The Oaks lounge drinking Cuban liquor from Michel's private locker. Someone sat down at the piano by the bar and began a run-through of "It Had to Be You."

"This is the last of the anejo I had shipped up from Miami," Michel said, eyeing the amber liquid. The others, faces and white hair softened by lamplight, set their stemmed glasses on the low table. Murmured comments about the new carpeting in the lobby, the increase in monthly fees, fell away. Michel broached the topic that was on all of their minds.

"How was your lunch with Nahum?"

Anna tried to brighten. "It was good seeing him." They would love to learn that Nahum and his wife had talked to a lawyer about a possible discrimination suit against The Oaks. They would be stunned to know he was raped. Interested to know the depth of his anger against his brother-in-law. She moistened her throat with the rum. "We always have a great deal to talk about." She didn't mention that their lunch was a failure; that, as they'd mumbled an apology and stumbled back to the car, the waitress ran after them, asking if they wanted to change their order.

"What does Nahum say about his brother-in-law?" Georgina prodded.

"And what does he plan to do?" asked Orville.

There was nothing more Anna wanted to say, but because they'd commandeered a dinner table for four and now, post-dessert, were hosting drinks, she felt she owed them something.

"Charges against Nahum have been dropped," she summarized, "and he's resuming his life. He has a job interview next week." They wanted more. Looking into their upturned faces, she longed to retreat to her apartment and avoid this hunger for information and gossip.

"Is he interviewing with another retirement home?" Orville asked.

"I have no idea," said Anna. She changed the subject. Choosing Michel as the likeliest target, she said, "Did you and your wife ever consider staying in Florida for your retirement, Michel?"

But he didn't take the bait. "No," he said. "It was time for the Florida chapter to end." His failure to elaborate surprised all of them.

"Do you ever think of going back to Florida?" Georgina asked.

"Never," he said in a swift expulsion of certainty. "Miami is in the past. More anejo?" Like children who sense a change in their parent but lack language to say so, they held out their glasses for refills, watching the stream of liquor with unwavering eyes.

Chapter Twelve

When Georgina and Orville pushed back their chairs and said they were going upstairs to bed, Michel stood, too. "We'll see you tomorrow," he called after them. Resting his hand on the back of Anna's chair, he said, "Why don't you stay a while longer?"

The pianist had begun "Hello, Young Lovers." The haunting melody was soon drifting among the seniors who had lived through romance, love, heartbreak and, in some cases, were now beginning their second or third trip through the cycle.

Seated again, he lifted his glass, revealing a starched white shirt cuff punctuated by an elegant mother-of-pearl cuff link. Though she would rather be alone in her apartment, it was nice to hear piano music while having her glass refilled by an attentive male.

"I understand you play the piano," he said, leaning toward her.

"Yes, I do," she said, wondering who had told him. She couldn't remember ever playing for anyone at The Oaks.

"I hope you'll play for us sometime."

"I'm not sure how many people want to hear Bach," she said. "Of course, I could bring sheet music for Rodgers and Hammerstein."

"Gershwin," he said. "And how about Bernstein?" He hummed a snatch of "Maria."

She smiled. "A wonderful song."

"I enjoy the weekly films and entertainments here at The Oaks," said Michel. "If I still had my car, I'd drive to the productions at the university. Perhaps," he added wistfully, "to St. Louis or Kansas City. In Miami we had season tickets for everything."

The pianist modulated into a new key.

"My sister was a cabaret singer," he volunteered.

"In Florida?"

"Miami. New York. You name it. Over the years, my wife and I heard her in several cities. She was a stunning performer. Wonderful musician." He shook his head. "You can read about her."

"I'm not as familiar with cabaret as I'd like to be," Anna said.

"The American songbook," Michel said. "Jazz and popular standards. I wish you could have heard her."

Anna didn't want to ask why he was using the past tense.

He swirled his drink. "I have her recordings."

"What is her name?"

"Her stage name was Angelique de Navarre. She died several years ago." Shaking his head as if death were utterly unnecessary, he said, "What a waste. One of these days I'll play you my favorite recording, *Angelique at Club Noir.*"

His profile, silhouetted in the lamplight, was exposed. She'd never actually studied his face, probably because she was always busy listening to him. Prominent cheek bones, high forehead, aquiline nose slightly slanted to one side, strong jaw. How had she not noted his features before?

He'd begun talking again. Frustrated by toggling between his looks and his words, she redirected attention to the anejo. Taking it as a cue to refill, Michel picked up the bottle. "Angelique is—was—a tall, beautiful woman with more talent in her little toe than I have in my entire body." Anna looked up.

"No, it's true," he insisted.

She hadn't disagreed.

He poured more rum and swirled his drink. "I tagged along with her to the neighborhood bar when our parents worked at night. She'd lift me onto a stool at the end of the bar and give me a sketch pad and colored pencils while she sang. The bartender fed me fruit drinks and salted nuts, and when she finished her set, my sister sat beside me and smoked and drank and ate salchichon from the kitchen."

"You're not Cuban, are you?" Anna asked.

"French," said Michel. "*Angelique. Michel.* Miami had a lot of Cubans, but quite a few French and Cajuns, too. It was a colorful place to live."

"Missouri must seem pale by comparison."

Michel shrugged his shoulders in what looked to Anna like an exotic gesture, Gallic, perhaps. Cajun. Creole. She was about to consider the subject of mixed heritage and how being the little brother of a cabaret singer named Angelique de Navarre might have shaped him, when he said, "Angelique had some of the best gigs in the business. She was always in demand." He paused. "In a way, you could say I never stopped being the little brother who followed her from show to show, always sitting on a stool at the end of the bar with a sketch pad."

The pianist had finished playing. The lounge was clearing out.

"Am I keeping you?" he asked, looking around before continuing. "My sister hit a rough patch. She was getting older. She wanted a family and never found the right guy. Never had a child. She started on a downward spiral. I was married by then and trying to establish the gallery. I didn't know she was drinking too much, doing drugs to feel better and sing better. I learned later she needed money." He usually talked fast, without hesitation, but now his pace slowed.

"She fell in with some rough people. While my wife and I were courting art collectors, Angelique was trying to score and find a place to sleep at night." He opened a silver cigarette case, then closed it again. "No smoking," he said, replacing the case in a jacket pocket. "Times have changed." He looked at Anna frankly. "My sister, a woman in her forties by then, with a huge talent, a big heart, physical beauty—aging beauty, but beauty nonetheless—lost herself. Her self. Do you understand?"

The uncharacteristic melancholy in his face, even his use of a word she admired and hardly ever heard, *nonetheless,* transformed him into a Michel she didn't know.

"I don't understand her deterioration." He roused himself and faced Anna. "You're a woman, Anna. Can you explain it?"

Anna set her drink down and got to her feet. For a moment he'd shown depth. "Women deteriorate. Men deteriorate. Failure is failure."

He was looking up at her. Almost beseeching. "But she was talented. And beautiful. Men loved her."

"Did they treat her with respect? Did she respect herself?"

Michel transferred his gaze to the chandelier hanging from the center of the ceiling. "She was tempting."

"What do you mean?"

"She was a beautiful woman, Anna. Men couldn't ignore her."

"Maybe her good looks exhausted her," Anna said.

"What do you mean?"

"Maybe she wanted to be appreciated as a person, not just as a beautiful woman."

"Men will always be tempted by a beautiful woman. What woman doesn't want to be beautiful? What woman doesn't want to attract a man?"

Anna felt a sudden desire to return to her apartment, away from this conversation, away from Michel. He stood, subtly alarmed.

"Your sister must have been very unhappy," said Anna. "And I'm beginning to feel unhappy with what you say about her."

He was following her to the hall. "I apologize."

"Mindless assumptions," she interrupted. "Too much emphasis on women's looks." The elevator arrived with a ding. Without a word Anna entered it and ascended to the fifth floor, uncomfortably aware of Michel's courtly attention back in the lounge and how much she had enjoyed it.

Chapter Thirteen

"May we join you?" Philip asked the next morning as Anna was finishing her coffee in the dining room.

"We saw you in the lounge last night," Meg said, seating herself and glancing over the breakfast menu. "You and Michel seemed to find a lot to talk about."

"Have you ever known Michel *not* to find a lot to talk about?" Anna asked.

"Hah!" said Philip.

"By the way, how is Nahum?" Meg asked.

"Doing well."

"I understand he comes by now and then," said Philip.

"Not to my knowledge," said Anna.

"Oh? Friends of ours have seen him here."

"I talk to him every once in a while." Anna folded her napkin.

"They haven't filled his position yet, have they?" said Philip.

"Not to my knowledge."

"He was well-liked," said Meg.

Gossip had less effect on Anna than it used to. Chitchat in the dining room came more easily now. She was adjusting to life at The Oaks. Her health was improving. On her way up to the fifth floor, she wondered if she'd left Woodland Street too soon. But of course her house had been sold. 915 Woodland Street was now out of the question.

Yet, when she received a telephone call a half hour later, her tremor returned and she found herself needing the cane. It was Sebastian. He'd purchased a cell phone in order to talk long-distance. That alone, she knew, was a cry for help.

"Where are you?" she asked, sitting down.

"On the interstate. Just south of Chicago. With Heather." His voice faded and he had to repeat himself. "The guy on the internet stirred up all kinds of trouble for us."

Us had always meant Sebastian and Heather. Now Anna had a curious feeling she was being included. "What kind of trouble?"

"Well, he roughed her up. She—"

Anna took a sharp breath. "What happened?"

"Assault."

"What kind of assault?"

He didn't answer.

"How long have you been in Chicago?"

"Several days. The gallery where she was supposedly going to exhibit doesn't exist. I couldn't find her." He grabbed a breath. "The guy on the internet *does* exist, and I can tell you he's a criminal."

The thought flashed across her mind: *another crime? Something else I can't imagine?* "Are you bringing her home?"

"We're on the interstate now. She's gone inside the gas station. She won't leave the pickup except for a quick trip to the bathroom."

"Has she been to a doctor?" *She was learning faster than she wanted to.*

"The ER released her"—his voice broke—"but she looks terrible."

"Come home, Sebastian," Anna said.

"I'm out of my depth," he said.

"Come home," she repeated. She ended the conversation because she sensed he couldn't.

The swell of sympathy she'd controlled during the phone call broke through. Frightened, energized, she emptied the dryer, folded clean clothes and linens, then went into the kitchen to heat up the teakettle, as if a pot of tea could hasten Sebastian and Heather home.

Hours later Sebastian, alone, picked her up at The Oaks. Driving to the warehouse through the wet afternoon, he stared glumly into the rain-spattered windshield. The beat of the wipers was like a pulse. It dawned on her that he wasn't telling her what happened in Chicago because he didn't really know. Anna pictured the two of them seated on either side of Heather's bed, begging for information.

Sebastian's below-ground-level space allowed light through high windows set just under the ceiling. Anna had always enjoyed his bohemian studio-residence, but now she wondered if Heather didn't need fabric rather than concrete, upholstered chairs instead of stools, appliances rather than a hot plate.

A mother and a father instead of a single dad.

Sebastian leant Anna his arm as they descended the back steps from the parking lot. Behind the cement wall, she knew, were rows of shelving that held his pottery. Wedged between another wall and a table was his daybed. Farther back, the wheel. In a corner, bags of wet clay.

"Does she know I'm coming?" Anna asked.

"Yes. I'm always open with her." But the usual sense of pride in his parenting principles sounded hollow. Heather's trauma in Chicago had cracked his world. Anna's world, too, was affected. Gone the fright-fueled strength she'd felt after the phone call earlier. Gone the recharged heart rapidly pumping blood around her eighty-year-old system.

The table was set for three. The daybed held pillows and an afghan. "I've tried to make it inviting," he said, closing the door and locking it behind him.

"You lock the door now?"

Sebastian shrugged. "She wants it locked." He pushed aside a narrow curtain covering a closet and hung their damp jackets on a clothes rod.

"When did she eat last?"

"On the interstate. A hamburger and fries." He bent to the small refrigerator and pulled out chicken and a container of cooked rice. "I thought we could make stir-fry." Anna set down a bread pudding she'd brought from home. Busy rinsing vegetables, pouring oil into a wok, they didn't see Heather come out of her room, stand barefoot in the concrete floor's thin layer of studio dust, rest her left foot on top of the right before reversing the process, silently watch them from the eye that wasn't swollen shut.

Anna turned and reached for a cutting board. "Oh, God," she whispered. At her intake of breath, Sebastian looked up. In the silence, rain rattled on the high windows and ran in rivulets down the darkening glass. Heather walked to the daybed and sat on the edge, her knees under the table, her arms folded. Anna continued working at the sink.

"Cup of tea?" Sebastian asked.

Heather nodded yes before lying back on the pillows and pulling the afghan over herself.

The wok's spattering sounded almost cheerful. Even Heather responded to the sizzle of hot oil, the smoky plume, and sat higher against the pillows. The electric teakettle began to whistle. Later, when they'd taken their places at the table, Anna and Sebastian leaned forward, almost consciously offering their own warmth along with the food.

"Some stir-fry?"

Heather picked at her plate while Sebastian served the rice. Anna ate steadily, aware of the girl laying her fork on the plate and leaning back against the pillows. Gone was the young woman whose spiky confidence once dominated conversation. In fact, there *was* no conversation. Rain drummed on the windows and the tea water simmered.

"Want to come with me while I drive Anna home?" Sebastian asked his daughter when the dishes were done. Heather turned her face into the pillows without answering.

"I'd like for you to visit me sometime," Anna said a few minutes later, going to the clothes rod for her jacket. To her astonishment, and apparently Sebastian's, Heather lifted her head.

"Can I come now?"

"Of course," said Anna.

Heather slid out between the daybed and table and went toward her room, past the bags of clay and the industrial vacuum cleaner standing at the doorway. The hem of her flannel granny gown fell just above her bare feet.

Sebastian leaned back against the sink, his expression blank. "I guess she can watch TV at your place," he said, as if there wouldn't be enough for his daughter to do. "She'll like that," he added. He'd never furnished the studio with a television. "She didn't bring her computer back with her."

"Maybe the three of us can talk a bit," Anna said.

Sebastian cocked his head. "She may not be ready."

"Has she told you what happened?"

He shook his head no.

"Where was she when you found her?"

"In the ER."

The hospital, she thought, *where you didn't find me for days.*

"The cops called me," he said.

"How did they know—"

But he'd already left for the bathroom and was closing the door firmly behind him.

Privately, Anna thought the girl—no, the young woman—might want to talk about what had happened to her. Heather emerged from her room a few minutes later in sweat pants and jacket, her hair in a pony tail.

"Where's Dad?"

"I'm here," Sebastian said, returning. He took in her running suit. "Good choice. It's chilly out."

Heather adjusted her sleeves at the wrist, almost as if she had an interest in her appearance. But by the time they reached the parking lot, lit by a floodlight posted high at the back of the warehouse, she still hadn't spoken. She moved close to Anna, avoiding the stick shift as Sebastian backed out. Even after he threw the truck into first, second, then third, she stayed where she was, warming Anna on the way to The Oaks. Anna looked over at Sebastian, who was driving with an absence of thought, his face a mask. Now and then he wiped the fogged-over windshield with the back of his wool shirt sleeve. No one spoke.

As the down-shifting at stop signs and red lights jostled them against each other, Anna felt an unaccountable optimism, as if she were being carried home in a glowing lantern meant to guide and warm families that belong together, no matter what.

Chapter Fourteen

As they entered the lobby of The Oaks, Michel was just stepping off the elevator. Watching him approach their three solemn figures, Anna felt almost amused at his speechlessness. She stepped aside, out of his path. Heather scooted into the elevator before the doors could close, Sebastian behind her, while Michel kept his head down on the way to the dining room. Shocked by Heather's swollen face and black eye, he would no doubt tell Georgina. Before long, Meg and Philip would be knocking on her door.

"We can sit in the living room," Anna said, clicking on the light and closing the apartment door behind her, "or we can go in the study." With its sofa bed, the study could serve as Heather's bedroom if she wanted to stay overnight. It was also the TV room. Here, she could watch as much television as she wanted.

"Coffee?" Anna asked. No one wanted coffee. While Heather and her father filed into the study, Anna hung jackets in the coat closet, then followed them down the hall. The girl had found a quiz show rerun, though after Sebastian patted the cushion and gestured for Anna to join them, all three sat staring at the screen without interest, detached from the laugh track and applause. They endured the beginning of a commercial before Sebastian leaned forward and moved a stack of magazines in search of the remote control. But Heather was already pointing it toward the television. Pale, speechless, her black eye swollen, she was in pathetic charge of the mute button and not much else.

TV, computer, smart phone, Anna thought. *How sad Heather looks.*

"I'm so glad you got away," she said impulsively, peering around Sebastian and speaking directly to Heather. "It couldn't have been easy."

Sebastian's face drained of expression. Heather stared at Anna who did not flinch, even though her remark had released high voltage into the room. Sebastian stood. He couldn't endure talk about Heather and Chicago.

"It must have been difficult," Anna continued, turning to face Heather directly and ignoring Sebastian as he left the room.

Heather seemed almost paralyzed. Damage was visible. It wasn't only the black eye. Her face looked puffy, almost water-logged. The skin was gray, and even the good eyelid seemed heavy and slack.

"Would you like to see a doctor, Heather?"

"I already did. Where's Dad?" And she stood and left the room.

A few minutes later, Sebastian was back in the doorway, wearing a baffled expression. Anna got up from the sofa and followed him back to the living room where she caught up to him at the door.

"I'm sorry," she said, not yet deeply sorry, believing that he was too private and that Heather needed to talk about Chicago. Neither father nor daughter said good-bye as they zipped up their jackets on the way out.

Anna closed the door, leaned against it for a moment, turned off the light, and slowly made her way back along the hallway to the bedroom, remorse building with each step. She'd said too much. She should have let Heather bring up Chicago when she was ready.

Dressing for bed, Anna glimpsed herself in the mirror. Unlike artistic representations of old women depicted with determined appreciation—sculptures, paintings, photographs—she observed her sagging breasts, withered flanks, bristling hairs under her arms and loose stomach—a naked old woman without the charm of art. As she stood beside the bed in her nightgown, she felt a sick flooding in the lower basin of her pelvis where memories of sex, regeneration, birth still lingered.

"Heather," she groaned, lying down and pulling the covers over herself. She had pushed the girl too hard. She turned onto her side. The spring night beyond the sliding screen door brought no pleasure. The narrow balcony and two porch chairs irritated her. Falling asleep would not be easy. She imagined Heather lying open-eyed in her bed, afraid of her thoughts, afraid of the man who had tracked her from a Missouri warehouse to an artists' collective in Chicago. Turning onto her other side, she closed her eyes against the abrasive light shining from the "Help" button in the bathroom.

A mourning dove's run-up to a three-note lullaby slipped through the screen, the repeated fragment full of melancholy.

Chapter Fifteen

Next morning as Michel approached her at the little lock boxes in the mailroom, Anna felt a disturbing inclination to confide in him. Remembering the letter he'd written to The Oaks management on behalf of Nahum, recalling the tender feelings for his sister, she almost forgot his incessant chatter. And of course there was his talent. Anna was attracted to talent.

Still, Heather's experience in Chicago was none of this man's business. She would try to be as private as Sebastian.

"How are you, Anna?" Without waiting for an answer, he continued. "I was alarmed to see Sebastian's daughter yesterday."

"Yes," said Anna, concentrating on the combination lock.

Michel swung open the door to his box. "I knew the art world was rough, but I didn't know it was that rough."

Anna sorted through her mail.

"Is she staying with you?" Michel asked.

"No."

"She lives with her father?"

She didn't answer. She wouldn't be surprised if he asked how soon Heather planned to return to the city, whether she'd found a niche in the art world, how she'd gotten a black eye and bruised face. Anna stepped toward the lobby.

"Nice seeing you again," he said, turning away in the direction of his apartment. "Oh, by the way," he said, abruptly pivoting, "when is Heather returning to the city?"

Anna held back a smile. "I'm not sure."

"Well, when she's feeling better, I'd like to hear about the Chicago art world. By the way, how did she get the black eye?"

"You'll have to ask her," said Anna. "Or Sebastian."

"Well, nice to see you," he repeated, and proceeded toward the south hallway.

Just before noon, Nahum entered the lobby with a spring to his step. As planned, Anna was waiting for him in a chair near his old office. Management had asked him to return to The Oaks.

Anna smiled warmly as they gravitated toward the dining room. "Nahum, it's wonderful to have you back."

He held her chair as she seated herself at a corner table for two. "Vicki and I are discussing The Oaks offer."

"Did they apologize?"

"Not in so many words."

"I can almost forgive them," she said.

"Vicki's not so forgiving. I'm ready to get back to work, but she can't forget what they did to me."

"How is her brother?"

"Waiting for trial."

"And the girl?"

"In a shelter, I think." During the dense silence that followed, Nahum reached across the table. "How is Heather?"

"Not good."

"At least she's not in a shelter," Nahum observed. "She has her father and you." Unspoken was the contrast between Heather and the victim of his brother-in-law's trafficking. Anna was ashamed; she'd given little thought to the girl.

"There's no point in pretending I haven't overstepped the line with Sebastian's daughter," she said, and told him about what had happened in her apartment the evening before. "And of course with Sebastian."

"They'll forgive you," Nahum said, sitting back. "They need you."

"Will they?" She wanted to be needed. For half a century she'd been family-less. Tears gathered. "I need to see Sebastian."

"He's probably overwhelmed with his daughter's situation."

"Shall I just wait and watch?" Anna whispered.

"Yes," said Nahum.

"But it's only natural that I would want to know what happened," she defended herself.

"Yes," agreed Nahum. "And I have no doubt someone will tell you."

"Who? When?"

"I don't know. Try to wait." He smiled. "Until you can't."

I can, she thought. *I can wait.* She'd waited for Sebastian time and again. She accomplished a great deal while she waited, but when he came knocking, she usually set everything—books, computer files, her life—aside.

"Sebastian seems to require solitude on a regular basis," Nahum observed.

"Yes, especially when he's perplexed."

"That would be now."

"Indeed that would be now."

Nahum looked up with a frank inquiry. "He stayed with you after your accident, didn't he?"

"Many weeks."

"He was there when you needed him."

"He surprised me. I think that's when I realized he loves me." Though the rest of the dining room seemed surrounded by light and air, her corner felt airless. "Thoughts of the other driver hardly ever leave me," she confessed.

Nahum didn't try to minimize the horror. Did not say, *"He was talking on his cell phone, Aunt Anna,"* or *"He could have stopped, too."* They both knew she'd run the stop sign. She lowered her head. "Sometimes I can imagine how my husband felt."

"Sometimes I think about your little daughter," Nahum said. "I could have had a cousin all these years."

Anna recoiled, stung. His words released fresh grief. Yet in another way, she was comforted. Someone besides herself missed Marianna.

If she had only comforted Heather last night instead of blundering into the subject of Chicago. After a prolonged silence during which she struggled up from self-incrimination, she asked, "Does Vicki see her brother often?"

"He comes over to the house every few days. But of course," he added with self-control, "that will end soon."

"You wouldn't do well with a Sebastian in your life," Anna murmured, off-subject.

"No," he agreed, "I wouldn't. I like seeing Vicki every day and night."

"It's not working for me as well as it used to," said Anna. She felt a heart palpitation and, because Nahum was watching her closely, wondered if she'd lost color. "You can always go home to Vicki," she whispered.

"Yes," said Nahum. "And while you can't go home to Sebastian, I predict that he'll come home to you in a short time, and maybe bring Heather with him."

"Sebastian's home is in the warehouse," she said.

"Do you really believe that?" Nahum repositioned his silverware. During her silence he said, "You'll hear from him soon."

Chapter Sixteen

"My daughter likes your bread pudding," Sebastian said over his cell phone a week later.

"It's my grandmother's recipe," said Anna. "Would Heather like me to make another one?"

"I think she would," said Sebastian.

"With or without raisins?"

"The way you made it before."

"With." She thought for a minute. "Do you want to pick it up, or what?"

Sebastian's silence held suspense. "She wants to visit you," he finally said.

"Oh. Well, yes. Certainly."

"She's afraid to drive."

Giddy pleasure bubbled up through Anna's week-long emptiness. "Why don't you both come over this afternoon or evening. It doesn't take long to make a pudding."

"How about seven tonight?"

"Good."

"Do you need anything?"

"You and Heather."

Later, while twilight was settling outside among budding tree limbs and the bread pudding cooled on the dining room table, Sebastian knocked twice and opened the door, closely followed by Heather. Anna met them in the center of the living room, tempted, as usual, to babble when Sebastian brought his stillness into her world. At such times she was likely to say something silly, like, "Ah, the soldier back from the wars," or "To what do I owe this pleasure?" All of the possibilities flitted through her mind, including a ludicrous scenario—Question: *"To what do I owe this pleasure?"* Answer: *"My raped, trafficked daughter is hungry for your bread pudding with raisins,"* at which point Anna appears in a crisp apron and oven-pinked cheeks with the delicious and tender cure for sexual assault: a warm pudding.

But what she finally said was, "Hello."

Heather had brushed her hair out and wore Levi's and a bright sweater. Clean-shaven, Sebastian's face was weathered but enduring. "How've you been?" he said, and bent to kiss her cheek. Heather sat down in a corner of the sofa where Sebastian joined her after first strolling to the table.

"Very nice," he said of the pudding, and smiled what seemed to be his first full smile since returning from Chicago. He sat down and stretched his arm along the back of the sofa. "We made it out of the warehouse today."

"Where did you go?"

"To the grocery store," said Sebastian. Heather looked bored. "And the laundromat," he added. "How are things at The Oaks?"

"The same. Reliable." Anna folded her hands in a bland gesture. "You can count on The Oaks being pretty much the same from one day to the next."

"That, I can believe."

"There is one welcome change," she said. "Nahum has been asked to return to work."

Sebastian brightened.

"But he hasn't decided whether to accept the offer."

Heather leaned forward and picked up a magazine from the coffee table.

"There's a new issue of *Craft* on my bed," Anna said, "if you'd like to look at it." She and Sebastian exchanged their *oh-the*-Craft-*magazine* glance, amused contempt on his part, tolerance for tongue depressor art on hers.

"You, too, can have a sequined Easter basket," Sebastian said to his daughter, who smiled faintly. Both he and Anna were cheered by her reaction.

"If Nahum comes back," Sebastian said across the coffee table, "will he have the same position?"

"Yes, assistant director. And they've offered him a raise."

"Nahum is Anna's nephew," Sebastian explained to Heather, who showed no curiosity.

"Would you like some pudding?" Anna asked, beginning to move toward the table. "I forgot the coffee," she said as soon as they'd all seated themselves.

"Stay where you are," said Sebastian.

His familiar stride, the confidence he showed in her home, in her kitchen, in the full coffee pot waiting on the counter, flooded Anna with disproportionate happiness. With sudden intensity she loved not only

Sebastian, but her new apartment. Leaving Woodland Street had not been the end of everything after all. Happiness extended into old age; to The Oaks; to Sebastian's capacity for change; to Heather's doubtless recovery; to Nahum's return; to an essential resilience everywhere.

Heather sat hunched in her chair, looking, not at the pudding, not at Anna, not at her father returning from the kitchen, but at a vacancy above the table. Anna held on to her personal insight, this sense of joy. Her previous insensitivity was lamentable but hardly the end of the world. Sebastian poured coffee. Heather and Anna accepted his service. He nodded to Heather, who began dishing up the pudding. Not a word was spoken. Not a word needed to be spoken.

"Thank you, Anna," Sebastian eventually said. "It's very good."

By the time the pudding was finished, Sebastian appeared ready to leave. Turning to Heather, he said, "Ready?"

Heather looked undecided.

"Do stay," said Anna.

"I guess so," Heather said. Anna would have liked for Sebastian to stay, too, but was not surprised when he declined. Perhaps both father and daughter wanted some space between them. An invisible timetable went into effect: Sebastian returns to the warehouse. Heather moves into the study. Anna tidies up the kitchen. Early evening ends and nighttime begins, preordained.

After asking Heather if she needed anything, Anna continued on to her bedroom, showered, shook out a nightgown and robe, and walked onto her little balcony. A night draft slipping under the eave rippled her hair and nightclothes.

"Anna?" Heather said from the doorway. Anna turned and stepped back inside. "Can I talk to you?"

"Of course you can. Where would you be most comfortable?"

"Here," said Heather and dropped into the upholstered chair across from Anna's bed, giving Anna little choice but to position herself on top of the bedspread, her back against two pillows and the headboard. She'd learned her lesson and waited for Heather to speak. But the silence in the bedroom felt long and intricate, and she began to wonder if she should initiate conversation. She didn't know how.

"Dad isn't doing very well," Heather finally said.

"Oh?" Anna said.

"He stays up most of the night and sleeps all afternoon."

"His hours have always been a little erratic," Anna said.

"He might be having a breakdown," said Heather. The skin around her damaged eye had turned lavender and the bruises still discolored her temple and hairline. "Some kind of crisis," she added in a professional tone. "I haven't mentioned my concern to him yet. I thought I'd talk to you first."

"I haven't seen him much lately."

"I know you haven't," Heather said. "That's why I wanted to bring it to your attention."

"Could it be a reaction to the trouble in Chicago?"

"I don't think so," Heather said. "Maybe it's a midlife crisis."

"He's a little old for a midlife crisis, isn't he?" said Anna.

"You'd know more about that than I would," said Heather. Her recovering eye closed for a moment. "Did he sleep through the night when he stayed with you all those weeks?"

"Yes, I believe he slept well, except to help me when I needed the bathroom. Sometimes we talked late at night."

"What about?"

"You, among other things. He was concerned about being away for such a long time."

Heather shrugged. "Oh, he didn't need to be concerned about me. I was perfectly fine. I can take care of myself."

What? Anna thought. *Do you realize what happened to you in Chicago?* Then, silently, *Please help me understand what happened in Chicago.*

"Dad raised me to be independent," Heather continued in a stream of words that sounded almost hypnotic. "After all, how many people are raised in a warehouse and live to tell about it?" She laughed. "Yet he's very protective. It's always been like that." She tucked a strand of hair behind one ear. "Some of my friends fight with their parents all the time. They get in trouble. I stay out of trouble. Dad's and my life is peaceful. He likes his space and he gives me mine. We get along.

"But lately he sits and stares. And, like I said, he goes to sleep in the afternoon and stays awake at night. When I go back to Chicago, he'll be alone again and that's when he'll really need you." She leaned forward. "Will you keep an eye on him?"

"You plan on going back to Chicago, then?"

"Yes, as soon as I think Dad's crisis has passed. I'll let you know before I leave."

"I'm a little worried, Heather."

"Me, too."

"I'm concerned about you as well as your dad."

"Naturally, Dad wants me to stay here, but I have to live my own life." She kicked off her shoes and crossed her legs. "Do you still have your car, Anna?"

"Yes. It's parked in The Oaks garage. I like having it available for friends to drive me if I can't get a ride from your dad or The Oaks van."

"Would you let me borrow it?"

Anna paused. "No, I don't think so."

Heather turned away sharply, then bent to pick up her shoes.

"Do you have any suggestions," said Anna, groping for rapport, "how I can help your dad?"

"You can always make him a bread pudding," Heather said with more than a touch of impudence.

"Sure. I can do that. But nothing will help him as much as knowing you're happy."

"His pottery helps," said Heather.

"His pottery," agreed Anna.

"He's an artist," Heather said, standing abruptly.

"And so are you, Heather. Are your paintings in Chicago?"

Holding her shoes in one hand, the fleshy eye still lavender with injury, she stared at the foot of Anna's bed. Suddenly she dropped the shoes, covered her face with her hands, and collapsed back into the chair.

"You're an artist, too," Anna repeated, pushing herself off the bed and approaching Heather. "It's important to remember you're an artist." She reached out to touch the girl but was rebuffed. "Let's bring your paintings back from Chicago," she continued, leaning against the foot-board of the bed. "We need your dad's truck. A car won't hold them all."

"I'll never go back for them," Heather whispered.

"Are they in a gallery?"

"No."

"Do you know where they are?"

Heather struggled for a moment before crying out. "Burned!"

Anna took shallow breaths, as if deep ones might subtract from the air Heather needed. "Have you told your father?"

Heather shook her head no.

"Where was the fire?"

Heather sobbed fiercely. "In a barbeque pit! The day before Dad got there!" Her wet face was turned up toward the lamp. "They put the ashes in my suitcase."

"Who did?"

"Eldon and the others."

Anna tried to imagine men around a fire, ashes overflowing a suitcase, grit and flecks of art stuck in the zipper. She could picture a barbeque pit but not the men.

"There was a grill," Heather cried. "In the backyard. Brick. The size of a dog house. I had to watch! I watched them crack my canvases and poke them into the fire!"

Why can I imagine cracked canvases but not Heather's violated body?

"Heather, where were you?"

"I told you. In the backyard."

"No, I mean—"

"In a house."

"Have you told your father about this?"

Suddenly, explosively, Heather scooted to the edge of the chair. "I thought he liked my work! He liked me and he liked my work."

"Who?"

"Eldon!"

The room was growing chilly. Anna stepped away and closed the sliding glass door to the balcony. When she turned back, Heather was almost into the hallway. "He said he liked my work!" By now they were in the study. The girl, her face damp and mottled, sat for a moment on the edge of the sofa bed before falling back against the pillows.

"Can I get you some nightclothes?" Anna asked.

But as she dimmed the light, Heather cried out again. "The suitcase was new!"

Bending over the bed, Anna cupped the girl's overheated face between her hands.

"I thought he had a gallery," Heather whispered, and turned her head toward the wall. "By the way," she added tonelessly when Anna returned with the nightgown, "I didn't want to borrow your car so I could get my paintings. It wasn't that."

"I misunderstood," said Anna.

"It's because I don't want Dad to give me a ride every time I need to go somewhere."

"I imagine he's glad to," Anna said.

"That's just the point," Heather said, sitting up and placing her feet on the floor again. "I think he'd take care of me forever, but I really need to live my own life. He doesn't realize I can take care of myself."

Not in Chicago, Anna thought. Suddenly angry at Sebastian for thinking he could raise a daughter by himself in a warehouse basement, she watched Heather lie back down, swing her feet bed to floor, floor to bed, twice, three times.

"Until I know Dad's okay again," she finally said, "I won't leave." She began biting the cuticle around one thumb. "I'll paint some fresh work while I keep an eye on him."

"I'd love to see you get back to your painting," said Anna.

Over the phone a few days later Sebastian sounded shrill. "She won't leave the studio, even if I offer to go with her."

"Has she talked about what happened?"

"No," he said. "Truthfully, I don't want to know the details."

"*I* want to know," Anna said. "I want to know more."

"Have you asked her?"

Anna hesitated. "I'm afraid I find it difficult to talk to her."

"Would you consider coming with us to a pottery show in Louisiana?" he asked abruptly.

"Louisiana?"

"Louisiana, Missouri," he clarified. "Art town on the Mississippi."

"Absolutely yes," Anna said without admitting she thought he meant New Orleans. She would rather go to New Orleans. "Are you taking your pottery?"

"Yes. And I want Heather to see some of the galleries there. It's on the Mississippi," he repeated. "Maybe if you come along, she'll want to go."

"Is she painting again?"

"No."

"Has she started anything?"

Silence. Then, "She's recovering." His wish to close the conversation was clearly transmitted over the cell phone, which, she noticed, he was making use of more and more frequently. To call her. In unacknowledged desperation.

Chapter Seventeen

The city park a few blocks from The Oaks had come to life, forsythia past its peak, iris breaking through the cool ground, lilacs so close to blooming they almost had a heartbeat. Anna thought about the front and back yards of her old Woodland Street house, a visceral pang of homesickness thrusting up, like volunteers, through layers of the past. She didn't mention this Woodland Street homesickness to Sebastian sitting on the wooden bench beside her. It was a tender topic between them: Woodland Street, the closest thing they'd had to a home together.

Leaning forward on the bench, elbows on his knees, hands loosely clasped, he looked at her over his shoulder. "Ready to go back?"

No, she was not ready to go back, not ready to leave the greening grass and wisps of cloud blowing across the sky, but she hadn't made arrangements for return transportation on her own.

"Don't you want to get a little more fresh air?" she said.

"Yes, but not sitting on a bench."

The words stung. She wasn't moving well today. "Feel free to take a walk," she said, the phrase dragging a silent tail behind it: *take a hike.* "I'll wait for you here." But he had decided to leave. Standing, turning toward his truck, he remembered at the last minute to help her up from the bench and take her arm as she crossed the uneven ground.

Watching the shops on Main Street glide past, Anna was flooded by nostalgia for the life she'd led when she could flit to the university, to town, back home to Woodland Street. In those days she ate when she wanted, rested when she wished, and was quickly restored.

"Would you and Heather like to come over for a meal in the next day or two?" she asked.

"I'm not sure. We may be going back to Chicago," he said, "if I can pry her out of the studio."

"Oh?" said Anna.

"To talk to the police."

"I see."

"The guy was bonded out," Sebastian said bitterly. "I'm sure he's moved on by now. Heather hasn't told me very much about what happened."

"His name is Eldon," said Anna, "and he took her to a house across from a vacant lot with a brick barbeque the size of a dog house in back."

Sebastian looked at her with interest.

"That's what she told me."

"I know his name," Sebastian said after a sharp silence. "Remember, I hired a detective."

The car behind them honked. Sebastian ground the gears and moved forward. "Everything fell apart in Chicago," he exclaimed. "I'm trying to hold things together."

Anna twisted to look at him. "Things were falling apart before she left for Chicago."

"What do you mean?" he snapped.

"I've thought about it, Sebastian. This internet fellow must have had buyers lined up before she got there."

"So now you're an expert on the internet?"

"I don't mean buyers for her paintings."

"I know what you mean, Anna."

"I know a thing or two about men," Anna said, sounding fatuous even to herself. "They feel entitled to get what they want from women."

"I also know a thing or two about men. I know lots of them and not one is a pimp or rapist." He paused before blurting out, "You've never needed to protect yourself from *me*."

"Not physically. But you have no idea all the things men take for granted."

"No, *you* have no idea what happened to Heather! *You've* never been locked up and attacked and sold for money!" His anger made him flushed, then pale.

Anna sat silent, shocked by their vicious arguing. At age eighty, she was sitting in a truck, shouting. She lowered her voice. "But I've felt abandoned." He sucked in his breath. "Not after the accident," she quickly added. "You took wonderful care of me after the accident." How obtuse she was, female to his male. How obtuse they both were, cooking up a stew of credit and blame and trying to force-feed it to each other. "Men assume more power than they should," she finished, "and women let them do it."

Sebastian drove her home, stone-faced.

He's inadequate, Anna mentally stormed as she closed the apartment door behind her. *He visits me when he wants to. Holes up in his warehouse. Turns his back on others.*

But hadn't Anna tucked herself away at The Oaks, protecting herself from the world? Perhaps Heather inherited inadequacy, as if Anna and Sebastian were her parents, transmitting genes for restricted living.

How curious to think of Heather's mother, if you could call her the mother when all she'd done was provide a womb for nine months. *She* wouldn't have to accommodate herself to Sebastian or adjust to Heather. And Sebastian never had to adjust to Heather's—maternal container, womb-owner, baby-carrier. And Heather never had to adjust to two parents.

Anna turned on the radio. Bring on the world. Music. Politics. Human interest. She would try to forget about Sebastian and Heather. But almost immediately she snapped off the radio and went into the study filled with books, always her friends in distress. Slowing down, quieting herself, she began to read poetry, one rhythmic line after another: "As when one takes a walk into the woods..." *Reading seriously is pleasure,* she thought fleetingly, *yet hard work.* How much easier to be cynical, anxious, depressed than to freshen one's thoughts.

Sebastian, she admitted, was making an effort to adapt: accommodating his traumatized daughter. Adjusting to Anna, herself, eleven years older, half ill in her old age. How much easier for him if she were a younger, easygoing woman who never had automobile accidents or faced illness and approaching death. Of course, a younger, easygoing woman might drift away during his absences. Such a woman might find someone else. Maybe someone like Michel. Such a woman would have more fun than Anna. Such a woman would probably *be* more fun than Anna, too.

Michel was waiting in the lobby when she came down to dinner. Immersing herself in poetry had made her feel otherworldly. A little stupefied. Michel followed her to a table and, after coffee and dessert, invited her to join him in the lounge.

She followed him to a table near the bar and accepted a glass of liquor from his private locker.

"How have you been, Anna?" He smiled. "Can we summarize by saying you're thriving?" The smooth remark was a continuation of their table talk during dinner, a suave comment on her state of mind by a master of sociability.

"Moderately well," she answered. "And shall we say you're doing well, too?"

"Yes," he said, "I find the people at The Oaks congenial." A group of these congenial people entered the lounge laughing and settling themselves on bar stools. "Exhibit A," he said, gesturing. "But tell me," he said deftly, "how are things with your stepdaughter?"

To Anna's dismay, she began to tell him. Heather had run into some trouble, she said. Sebastian was concerned about her. The situation put Anna in a delicate position. She stopped as soon as she heard herself reach the end of a paragraph.

"Yes, I imagine it is difficult for you at times," he said, and Anna suddenly saw Sebastian as others might see him: in and out of The Oaks. Father to a daughter who had a black eye. Unreliable boyfriend.

"Sebastian is at a low point," she said, knowing she owed Michel no explanation. Still, she explained. "People here didn't know him when he was young, ignoring the success everyone else was chasing. He was original and unconventional. He still is."

"I take it you've known him for years," Michel said.

"Years and years," said Anna. "I know him very well."

"He's more than a friend, then?"

"Oh, yes." Earlier in the day she might have said he was less than a friend, but tonight she knew he was much more.

"So this difficulty that your stepdaughter finds herself in"—she decided not to correct him every time he said *stepdaughter*—"affects you as well as Sebastian and, of course, the young lady herself."

"Yes, it affects me," Anna agreed, omitting to add *profoundly*. "Do you have children, Michel?"

"No, I've never had children." He leaned back and assessed the level of anejo in his glass. "Half the time I'm sorry, and the other half I'm glad. It's my observation that having children is a crap shoot. Parents can do everything right and still fail with their children, and I've seen parents do everything wrong and their kids turn out well. Yes, indeed, I've seen some real problems with kids." He leaned forward. "The teenaged daughter of a friend of mine got involved with an older married man and it just about broke my friend's heart."

Anna bit her tongue. How easy to be pulled into a conversation she didn't want to have.

"We found out where they were," he said, "and brought the girl back."

Since she didn't want to learn anything more about Michel than she already knew, she continued to say nothing.

"This was before I was married."

"Many years ago, then," said Anna.

"Oh, many, many years ago."

Someone turned off the recorded music playing at a low volume throughout the lobby, dining room, and lounge. The withdrawal of sound resembled a momentary stumble. Anna almost reached out to prevent herself from falling.

"Her daughter was a constant source of disagreement between us and we eventually went our separate ways."

"What happened to the daughter?"

"I don't know," said Michel, refilling Anna's glass and then his own. "I'm guessing she got herself into another patch of trouble." He shook his head. "Some women can't say no."

Anna's cane struck the floor, softened by the carpeting. " Women don't get into a patch of trouble all by themselves. Let's skip the clichés."

Michel stared in surprise at her outburst. "I apologize," he said.

"Men are not entitled to sexual pleasure whenever they want it!" Anna said, struggling to her feet and beginning to move toward the elevators. Oh, how easily she could be flattered by an attractive man offering companionship, attention, and an after-dinner drink. When the elevator doors slid open, she stepped inside, pushed the fifth-floor button, and caught a glimpse of Michel walking away as the doors closed with a muffled sigh.

Chapter Eighteen

Approaching the mailroom on Monday morning, Anna saw Nahum's office door—the office door she'd never stopped thinking of as Nahum's—standing open. His family photographs were back on the top shelf of the bookcase; his tweed sports jacket hung on the coat tree again. She sat down in the lobby as if positioning herself at the main intersection of the world to watch him pass by.

"Did you see Nahum's office?" Georgina almost shrieked as she cut through the lobby on her way from the swimming pool. Her seventy-some-year-old dimples embedded in a face as pink as her swim bag almost blinked a light of their own. "He's back!"

Anna clasped her hands together and bowed her head slightly, indicating contentment.

"I can't wait to tell Orville!" Georgina sang out. "He'll be so surprised! Everyone will be surprised!"

As if on cue, Meg and Philip approached. "Have you seen your nephew's office?" Meg asked.

Anna nodded yes.

"Isn't it wonderful?" Georgina bubbled.

While Georgina and Meg stood talking, Anna got up and served herself at the coffee bar set against the wall. Returning through a flow of residents making their way to the dining room, she placed her cup on the table beside her chair and reflected on Nahum's departure and return, the shadow he'd passed through, the light he was stepping back into. But she knew from being Lorenzo's wife that The Oaks could turn ugly again. Any African-American assistant director would be more carefully watched than any White assistant director. And would he ever be director?

Nahum appeared beside the wingback chair. "Aunt Anna." He bent to kiss her cheek. "I was just up on the fifth floor looking for you."

"I've been down here waiting for *you*."

"Can you bring your coffee into my office?" She followed and waited while he turned the upholstered chair around and closed the door. Seating himself and taking her hand, he said, "It's very good to be back."

"I couldn't be more pleased, Nahum."

"And how are you and Sebastian and Heather?" His complexion was as smooth as butter. His eyes bathed her in warmth.

"A little stressed," she said with a half smile of regret. "But having you back makes everything nearly right."

He released her hand.

"Heather's frightened of being alone," she continued. "She's hiding in the warehouse. She's not painting, not going anywhere unless Sebastian goes with her. I think he's getting a little desperate."

"She's had a harsh experience," said Nahum.

"She won't talk about it. She doesn't even want to talk to the investigator."

"She needs to testify if the guy is going to be prosecuted," Nahum said.

"I doubt she's willing to do much of anything. She's sort of paralyzed."

Nahum touched the fingertips of both hands together. "After I was attacked, I got sick," he said. "You don't shrug off these experiences."

There was a knock at the door. Anna turned to look. "Heavens," she said, half rising. It was Sebastian.

Nahum was already on his feet. "How's it going?" he said, opening the door wide and extending his hand.

"Good to see you," said Sebastian. "Glad you're back." He nodded to Anna. Then, "Are you free for breakfast?" The question was for Nahum.

"Sorry, but I have a meeting this morning."

Sebastian turned to Anna.

"I'm free," she said. "Where's Heather?"

Sebastian rubbed his hand over his craggy face, forehead to chin. "Still sleeping."

"Nahum knows some of what's happened," Anna said. With Nahum, Sebastian was forthcoming.

"She's had a terrible experience in Chicago," he said. "And she's nothing like her old self." His cell phone rang.

"Hi ... I'm over at The Oaks ... I'll be back in an hour ... Okay, half an hour ... I left the door locked ... There's coffee in the pot. Have some cereal and ... By the time you're showered and dressed I'll be on my way back." He closed the phone and replaced it in the pocket of his flannel shirt.

"She's afraid." Nahum stated the plain fact, no question mark.

"Oh, yeah, no doubt about that." Sebastian sat down, leaned forward in his chair, then moved from side to side, trying to settle into one position. "She's afraid, all right."

"What happened in Chicago?"

Finally settling, Sebastian extended his long legs and work shoes. "The Chicago police called from the ER and said my daughter had been found during a raid, drugged. Dazed. She gave them my name. I drove to Chicago, picked her up, and drove her home."

"Are they following up with an investigation?"

"He was released on bond. We'll have to go back for the trial."

"Have they questioned her?"

"By phone. She doesn't want to talk to anyone."

"She'll have to," said Nahum, "if he's going to be put away." And that was all that was said. Sebastian drew in his legs, stood, and turned toward the door. Anna followed him out of the room.

At breakfast, conversation was all false starts and static. She thought he'd come as an apology for the dismal drive back from the park, yet he did not apologize. Chewing his food looked like an effort; conversation, an effort; being away from Heather, an effort; returning to the warehouse, an effort.

Over the years, she knew, Sebastian had endured more wordless effort than he ever would admit. She often tried to ease his discomfort. Dragging his dark thoughts out into the daylight was something she occasionally succeeded at. Granted, at times she overdid honesty and transparency. Sometimes she exaggerated his thundercloud of conflicts, only to find, while she probed, that his mind was actually skimming along, satisfied, in a private vein.

He left before finishing his first cup of coffee, a smear of half-eaten egg on his plate to remind her he'd been there at all.

Chapter Nineteen

On the way out of town the blue pickup truck with Sebastian, Heather, and Anna in the cab passed below the hospital, fortress overlooking the river. To Anna, it was the limestone presence that always cast shadows of her daughter's, her husband's, and the SUV driver's deaths. Three ambulances winding their way up the rock hill. No, four, counting the one she'd been in.

Today, though, she was distanced from the limestone by a soft rain falling like a gauzy curtain around the hospital walls. The humidity in the air made her white hair curl at the temples. From the moment she woke up, she'd felt strong. Climbing into Sebastian's truck had been easier than usual. She may not be going to New Orleans, but she was delighted to get away, even to Louisiana, Missouri.

And Louisiana, Missouri, pleased her as Sebastian approached the Mississippi River bridge and turned off just in time to avoid going over into Illinois. Inside the truck, the light patter of water on the roof and windshield softened the outside world. Sebastian parked at the river walk. In front of them, the Mississippi flowed, slow and deep and dimpled by the rain. Anna folded her hands, aware of warmth from Heather's shoulder on her left and cool, moist currents of air seeping through the passenger window on her right. Behind her, the seat back captured her own warmth; in front, the Mississippi flowed on. She felt alive in all directions.

"Ever been here before, Anna?" Sebastian asked, leaning forward against the steering wheel to peer around Heather seated in the middle.

"I've ridden across the bridge," Anna said, "but never parked on the river bank." Behind them, the town occupied its high ridge: small art galleries tucked between a bed-and-breakfast. A gift shop. Beauty parlor. Post office.

"I'm going to stretch," said Sebastian, opening the driver's door. "Want to get out of the truck?"

"I'll wait till it stops raining," said Anna.

"There's a shelter," he said, pointing his thumb, hitchhiker-style, to picnic tables under a roof farther along the walk. He stepped down onto the pavement. The door resisted, then closed with a rusty shriek.

As they watched him follow the low stone wall between sidewalk and riverbank, Heather leaned forward and tried to turn on the radio. "Oh. I forgot. He's got the key." The rain drummed on the truck and the windshield steamed over from their breathing. "Are you warm enough?"

"I'm fine," said Anna, as surprised by the considerate question as by the fact Heather had chosen to stay in the truck.

"It's good to have a little time away from Dad."

"Is he sleeping better at night now?" Anna asked.

"I don't think so."

"Is he making new pots? I thought he brought some with him today." Anna gestured with a nod toward the enclosed truck bed behind them.

"We packed them up," said Heather, "but they're not new. I haven't seen him do any new work lately."

"Do you have room to work in your dad's studio?" She'd rather say *room to work* than *room to paint*. Anna couldn't think of Heather's paintings without hearing the sound of cracking canvas, seeing a fire in a barbeque pit, ashes in a suitcase.

"Not really." Heather looked away from the river and down at her Levi's where a floral print patch stretched across a hole at the kneecap. "I'm looking for a studio of my own."

"Good," said Anna.

"There's some unused space next to my room."

Anna turned to look at her. "In the warehouse?"

"Yes. On the other side of my bedroom wall."

"Is it available?"

"I hope so."

The rain grew louder and dumped a heavy load of water onto the parked truck. Anna glanced at the shelter where Sebastian stood in profile, a stone presence himself, or maybe a prow, a ship's prow facing the river, a kind of maritime strength here at the Mississippi. Anna sat quietly. The silence in the truck slowly thickened. Suddenly, Heather's spasmodic breaths grew noisy. Throwing her head onto Anna's shoulder, she emitted a cry. Anna reached around and cupped the girl's face with her right hand, vaguely aware of Sebastian returning to the truck and turning aside when he saw, through the windshield, his daughter sobbing into Anna's shoulder. He stood without moving, oblivious to the sky's floodgate opening above him, rainwater pounding against his head and shoulders. He hesitated, then began walking back to the shelter.

"There, there," Anna said.

Eventually Heather's crying slowed. But instead of sitting up, letting air circulate between her damp, creased cheek and Anna's wet jacket, she remained where she was.

"Eldon was such a liar," she whispered, and had to endure a coughing fit.

"Yes," Anna murmured.

"He never intended to have an exhibit of my paintings."

"No, he didn't."

"He didn't even have a gallery." She sat up and looked at Anna. "He just wanted sex and money." She gulped for air. "Other men paid him..." Her voice cracked. "He complimented me, but he was lying." She broke into another storm of tears.

"He had plans even before he met you," Anna ventured, but pulled back from further comment when Heather grew defensive.

"I'm no different than anyone else! Everyone uses the internet!"

"Yes," Anna said.

"He sounded nice. He's good-looking in person. He has a lot going for him."

"Except integrity." Anna heard how old-fashioned the word must sound.

Heather returned to Anna's shoulder. The gesture itself burrowed through Anna's jacket, into her flesh, all the way into her heart. She rested her cheek on top of the girl's head and waited for Sebastian to return to the truck.

"Men are horrible," Heather said.

"Some are."

"Eldon is the worst of all. I hate him and I hate his name."

"I hate the name, too," said Anna.

Heather shot up so fast her head almost cracked against the top of the cab. "I want you to hate *him*, Anna!"

"I do," Anna assured her.

Heather rested her head against the seat back and closed her eyes. Tears were running down her face again, but this time soundlessly. "Do you ever think of something over and over again and the more you try to stop thinking about it, the more you think about it?"

"The accident," said Anna. "My accident. The more I tried not to think about it, the more I thought about it."

"For how long?"

"A long time." Anna leaned back. "I saw myself leaving the house, locking the front door behind me, getting into my car parked in the driveway. That's how the movie always starts. Then I try to change the details, like make the car go the other way on Woodland Street, away from the stop sign at the intersection. Or I try to slow everything down. Or sometimes I invent a neighbor coming out of her house and waving me over to her yard. 'Come in for a cup of coffee,' she says, and I get out of my car and go inside her house. When I come back out, I decide not to drive to town after all. Anything to avoid what really happened. But then eventually I stopped going over and over the imaginary scenes."

Heather had grown still. "He made movies," she whispered.

"What do you mean?"

"It's on film."

Once, Anna had seen a few minutes of a pornographic film, astonished, not by the sexual content, but by the primitive screenwriting, acting, and camera work. She remembered laughing and changing the channel because, ultimately, she was bored.

That film was sold for money, broadcast, she supposed, to profit the television station, the producers, advertisers, agents, film writers—if, contrary to all evidence, there were any—camera crew, actors. Were the actors paid to display themselves and their private functions? Promised something? Stardom, maybe? A modeling career? *Force, fraud, or coercion.* One of the girls in the film looked very young. To Anna, her phony orgasms seemed like disguised cries for help.

"Did you just tell yourself to stop?" Heather was saying.

"Stop what?"

"The movie in your head."

"Your dad helped me," Anna said.

"How?"

"He was there to talk to. I could use my voice to say ordinary things."

"I can't talk to anyone," Heather admitted.

"Talk to me if you can," Anna said.

"Men may have nice faces..." She trailed off.

"We have to get used to bodies slowly," Anna said. "For you, it was too sudden. Too fast. And too many." She smiled. "One at a time, you know. Maybe one per lifetime."

Heather looked doubtful.

"And remember: these men didn't care anything about you. They were there for sensation. Eldon was there for money." Afraid that Heather would withdraw, she stopped talking.

The girl covered her face with her hands and forced words through her fingers. "Too many, yeah. Too fast. Animals. All hard and hairy and bad smells."

"You need everything slowed down," Anna said soothingly. "Some day, when you love a man and he loves you, and you're both kind, it will be different. It won't hurt. It will be good."

"He loved my paintings," Heather whispered after a silence.

"Yes, that's what he told you."

Her voice rose. "It was terrifying. They really hurt me. In every way." She looked up. "They're thugs."

"Thugs, yes."

"They belong in jail."

"I hope that's where they end up, Heather."

Heather gripped Anna's upper arm. "Dad says I have to testify. I have to go to court. But I'd have to look at them. I can't do that. And they'll come after me."

"You can move," Anna ventured. "They won't find you. You can stay with me—"

"I'll never be safe." She sat up. "Seeing their bodies will make me sick. *Seeing a man's body will always make me sick!*"

"It won't always make you sick," said Anna.

The driver's door screeched open and Sebastian climbed into the truck, dripping and smelling of damp flannel shirt. He sat with his hands on the top of the steering wheel, not speaking. In front of them, the Mississippi rolled on.

In court, Anna stupidly thought, *Eldon and the others will have their clothes on.* She stopped herself. *You may as well pretend the limestone hospital overlooking the river doesn't remind you that Marianna and Lorenzo and the driver of the black SUV died there. That you almost died there yourself. Neither you nor Heather can unknow what you already know.*

Chapter Twenty

All the way home from the Mississippi River, the pots in the back of the truck clinked in their packing materials. Anna was let off at The Oaks with a brief assist and taciturn good-bye from Sebastian. Heather waved once as the truck drove away.

Anna pushed open the heavy door, whose pneumatic whoosh swept her through the main entrance as impersonally as she'd been swept from the banks of the Mississippi. Except for the few minutes alone with Heather in the truck, the trip to Louisiana, Missouri, had failed. She knew Sebastian felt the failure as deeply as she. Perhaps more so. Seeing his daughter crying into Anna's shoulder, he locked himself into silence, barely speaking during the drive home. Could he not tolerate anyone drawing close to Heather? Was he simply overwhelmed by the damage done to his daughter? Anna's heart raced. *Damn you, Sebastian, for your privacy, your silences, your aloneness. And you, Heather, for your lack of experience. Your stupidity in Chicago.*

She walked past Michel who, pausing in the lobby, ready to exchange pleasantries, was reduced to surprised silence and a solitary trip into the dining room for dinner. Anna ate alone in her apartment. She was preparing to go to bed early when her phone rang.

"Hello, Anna," Michel said when she answered. "I found your number in The Oaks directory."

"Yes?"

"Will you join me for a drink in the lounge? I've had dinner. I take it you're eating in your apartment?"

"Yes, I am."

"If you're with Sebastian, why don't you both come down and join me."

"I'm alone," she said. "I'll be down."

Michel was sitting in the lounge at a cocktail table when she came toward him. He stood and touched her elbow in a steadying gesture. "Can I interest you in a drink?

"You chose a good evening not to eat in the dining room," he said, returning with two ruddy brandies. "The menu was disappointing."

"I was tired. I had a busy day."

"Oh?" said Michel, interested.

She hesitated. "I've been to Louisiana. The Mississippi River."

He lifted an eyebrow.

"Louisiana, Missouri." She took two cocktail napkins from him and laid them on the glass table while he cradled the brandy snifters.

"May I ask why?"

"Art."

"With Sebastian?"

"Yes. And Heather."

"Are there galleries in this Louisiana, Missouri?"

"Yes, but we didn't actually visit them."

"I see." He set the brandies on the tabletop. "Well, then, how was the Mississippi?"

"Deep and slow."

He seated himself and lifted his glass. "And what prevented you from visiting galleries?" He crossed one leg. She felt ridiculous for noticing that his knees were well shaped.

"Heather and I were talking in the truck. Sebastian was walking along the river and got caught in a rainstorm. We just didn't get around to the galleries." Aware of the wooden explanation, she took a sip, hoping the brandy would inspire her either to say something interesting or to stop talking. "Sebastian didn't like seeing Heather confide in me."

"Why is that?"

She'd known he would ask. Soon he would want to know what Heather confided and she would tell him.

"Sebastian and I have known each other a long time," she said. She and Michel could circle a target, whereas Sebastian could be nothing but straightforward or silent. For a moment she pitied him. "Sebastian is a unique person. Original. Somewhat solitary."

"So I gather," Michel said dryly.

"I've never been close to Heather."

"I see."

She swallowed brandy and waited for its scorch to subside. "Sebastian doesn't like to share Heather."

Michel's pupils were black points in faded irises that, at one time, must have been drop-dead blue. "He let her go to Chicago, didn't he?"

Anna hadn't expected him to take sides. Was this some sort of male solidarity?

"He didn't have much choice," she said. "Heather was determined."

"I gather things didn't go well for her there."

"Sebastian had to rescue her."

"From what?"

She glanced away and back again. "A situation not unlike the one with Nahum's brother-in-law."

Michel expressed no surprise. "It isn't as rare as you might think."

"Maybe not where you come from," Anna said, "but criminal sex is rare here. Or used to be."

He neither agreed nor disagreed.

"It's been terrible for Heather," she continued, leaning toward his armchair, "and terrible for her father. Imagine if she were your daughter." She wanted to criticize Sebastian, but here she was, turning him into a sympathetic figure.

Michel held his glass up to the light. "I don't have to have a daughter in order to imagine it."

A few swallows would finish off the brandy and she could go back up to her apartment, breathe new life into her resentment of Sebastian, and nurse it alone.

"I am not unfamiliar with fathers and daughters," Michel continued, setting down his glass, positioning it delicately by the stem. "I've observed them many times over the years. It can be a fraught relationship."

Fraught relationship? Where was frivolous, flirty, gossipy, shallow Michel? Just as she was opening her mouth to speak, she froze involuntarily: Sebastian was standing in the far doorway, watching her. Beside him, Heather waved.

"Hello, Mike," she said, striding across the room with her old brio.

"Heather," said Michel, "how are you? Nice to see you again." He was too socially skilled to show surprise, either at seeing her or at hearing himself called Mike. He pulled two more chairs up to the table.

"It's been a long time since we've seen you, Mike," Heather said. Except for a certain hectic quality, she seemed like her old self.

"Yes, indeed. How has the art world been treating you?"

She smiled broadly. There was no longer bruising on her face. "I'm learning the ropes," she said, taking a seat. Sebastian came up behind her and stood behind her chair.

"Art galleries are brutal," Michel said. "You can't make any money working with dealers."

"Yes, I'm finding that to be true."

"Tell me all about the city," he said, knowing full well her Chicago enterprise had failed. "Are you painting? Meeting artists?"

"My paintings haven't sold yet," she said, her face flushing deeply, "but they're being talked about. They're creating a buzz. Things look very good. I'll be returning to the city soon."

Watching Heather's forced confidence, hearing her lies, Anna tried to imagine why she and Sebastian were here at The Oaks.

"Can I get you a drink?" Michel said to no one in particular.

"Water," said Heather.

"Nothing for me," said Sebastian.

"Another brandy, please," said Anna. When Michel was out of earshot she turned toward Sebastian with studied detachment. "I wasn't expecting you."

His veiled gaze followed Michel's progress to the bar. "No, I guess you weren't."

"Dad's meeting Nahum," said Heather. "Can we go up to your apartment?"

Anna hesitated.

"It's better than Nahum's office," Heather added.

"I'll be up when I've finished my brandy," Anna said coolly.

"Your second?" said Sebastian.

"Yes, my second," she said. "Or is it my third? Fourth?" She shrugged. "You're meeting Nahum?"

"I sure didn't come to sit around the lounge and talk to Mike," he said.

"Why *did* you come?" But Michel was returning with a tray holding two brandies and a water.

"Are you sure you won't have anything?" he said to Sebastian.

"I'm sure."

Michel shrugged tolerantly while balancing tray and glasses, too polite to say *suit yourself.* Heather took a swallow of the sparkling water.

"Thanks, Mike," she said. Whereupon, seeing her father turn away, she set her glass on the table, stood, and followed him out of the lounge with breezy nonchalance.

"That was sudden," said Michel in a wry tone. "Were you expecting them?"

"No, I wasn't."

He seated himself again and swirled his brandy. "Apparently they can't stay away from you." He reached out and put an advisory hand on her arm. "You may not realize it," he continued, "but Sebastian needs you more than you need Sebastian."

"Do you think so?" she said, flattered.

"You can be sure of it," he said, leaning closer until they were almost touching. "But what you can't be sure of is whether he'll let you into his family." The man's physical closeness, intimate tone, bewitched her.

"Perhaps I'm not interested in belonging to a family," she said coquettishly.

"Oh, I think you are."

How perceptive he was. Here was a man who knew her, who was taking the trouble to know her. She had the impression he was about to toy with a lock of her white hair. Suddenly she wanted him to. With controlled pleasure, they studied each other's face until she momentarily forgot about Sebastian waiting upstairs. When she remembered, she felt no rush to join him. Her dalliance in the lounge was interrupted only when she saw Nahum approach.

"Nahum."

"Hello, Aunt Anna. How are you, Michel?"

"You're working late," Michel observed.

Looking like a man who doesn't know why he's been asked to a party, Nahum took a vacant chair. "Sebastian asked me to meet him here."

"He's upstairs with Heather," Anna said.

"They all had a long day at the Mississippi River," volunteered Michel.

"The Mississippi?"

"Louisiana, Missouri," Anna said.

"Have you ever been there before?" Michel asked Nahum.

"Should I have been?"

"Not necessarily," said Michel. "Can we get you something to drink?"

Anna wondered just how much liquor the man could dispense in one evening.

"Thanks, no," said Nahum, getting to his feet again. "I'll go up and see Sebastian."

Just then Sebastian and Heather returned to the lounge. Had Sebastian, brooding in her apartment five stories above, grown too restless to wait? His hair stood upright in wiry tangles, and the craggy face seemed to have reverted to original wild terrain. Approaching carefully, like a footsore man, he was followed by Heather, who took a seat and returned to the glass of sparkling water she'd abandoned shortly before.

As if it were common for people to appear, disappear, and reappear without explanation, Michel said to Heather, "I understand you visited some galleries along the Mississippi today." Anna, waiting for him to say something disparaging about galleries, was stunned when he added, "Have you thought of opening a gallery of your own?"

Heather looked guarded. Sebastian cocked his head.

But Nahum showed quick interest. "We've talked about opening a small gallery here at The Oaks," he said, "for residents' work."

"I have one or two pieces available," Michel offered gratuitously.

"We've thought about bringing in artists from town, too," Nahum added.

"That would be you," Michel said, turning to Heather. "You could exhibit your work. Maybe even help curate. With that experience under your belt, you'd be prepared to open your own gallery. Set your prices. Take first cut."

Sebastian's eyes were feverish. "But you object to galleries."

"I do, unless they're mine."

"I need to do some new work before I can exhibit," Heather said, warily looking up at her father before returning to the reduced ice and diminished sparkle of her drink.

"Fresh work is good," said Michel. "Now, in my case—"

"Heather's paintings were burned in Chicago," Sebastian interrupted at a low volume that forced the others to pay attention.

"What?" said Nahum.

"The pimp burned her paintings." Sebastian looked directly at Michel. "The guy ought to be shot."

"Don't look at me," said Michel lightly. "I don't burn paintings."

"No?" said Sebastian.

Heather set her glass down and bent forward at the waist, almost as if she were going to be sick.

"The police found the suitcase," Sebastian continued. "Ashes. Burned chunks of canvas."

Heather struggled to her feet and started out of the lounge, Anna close behind.

"I need to talk to you, Nahum," Anna heard Sebastian say behind her. "Alone."

From the doorway, she saw Michel rise, button the single button of his jacket, and make his way out of the lounge. Once through the doorway, he swerved past her toward his wing of The Oaks, appearing, she thought, somehow tainted and small as he continued on toward the south elevators.

"Mike!" Heather yelled, her face red, her feet aggressively apart on the flowered carpet surrounding the reception desk that had closed for the night. "Mike!"

Michel paused before performing a cool about-face.

Anna turned away from the bright lights of the lobby. "Let's go out on the sunporch," she said, trying to sound calm. The two followed her toward the falling-water sounds of the fountain she'd barely noticed since first moving in to The Oaks. They sat down at a circular table. Through screens that now replaced the storm windows, a night breeze toyed with the ceiling fan overhead.

"Apparently Sebastian has an agenda tonight," Michel murmured.

"You bet he does," Heather said.

"It's been a hard day," Anna commented, contemptuous of the cliche as soon as she uttered it. Feeling the occasional wayward spray blown from the fountain, breathing the too-sweet night fragrance of foreign honey-suckle invading Missouri's lawns, she turned to Heather. "I'm surprised to see you and your father here tonight." Fireflies banged against the screens.

"He wanted to talk to Nahum," Heather said. Through narrowed eyes, she aimed a lightning glance toward Michel. "Dad likes to keep people informed."

Since when? Anna thought. Then, answering her own question: *Oh. Since tonight when the two of you waited upstairs. What has Sebastian told you?*

"I wouldn't have expected your father to mention the burned paint-ings," said Michel. "He seems to be a very private man."

"He is," said Heather.

"You have photographs of the destroyed work, haven't you?" Michel continued smoothly. "You document your paintings, don't you?"

"If you want to use that word," said Heather.

"I remember one photo you showed me, rods of color in a row," he continued. "The painting was about music, wasn't it?"

Heather put her elbows on the table and leaned forward, her chin in the palms of her hands, her eyes smoldering. "Not about music, Mike. About choice."

"Whatever it was, you can paint it again. Who knows? It might be better the second time around."

Heather dropped her hands to the tabletop with a slap. "I shouldn't have to paint it twice."

"Sometimes an artist has to paint a thing over and over again," he said. "You could look at this whole Chicago experience as a chance to paint new, better pictures. You could even say the guy turned you into an instrument for your art."

Heather stared, dumbfounded. "A *damaged* instrument!"

Michel's shrug was visible in the near-dark.

Have you forgotten about your sister? Anna thought.

Jumping to her feet, forming a tense missile aimed across the table, Heather began to let loose fury. "They had no right to do what they did! Don't talk about the men and my paintings in the same breath! They ruined me! They ruined my work!"

"Nonsense," Michel said. "You're not ruined. An artist endures pain for the sake of her art." He leaned back, cool, enigmatic, while Heather continued the attack, growing increasingly energetic, opinionated, and *alive*.

"It will take *years* for me to produce what they destroyed in a few minutes! My paintings will never be the same. *I'll* never be the same!"

Before Michel could retort, Anna said in clipped syllables, "How many artists do you know who've been assaulted, Michel? Sold? Their work destroyed?"

"Several, as a matter of fact. Several, Anna. And I've seen artists refuse to be ruined. In fact," he added in an aloof afterthought, "you're looking at one."

"How have you refused to be ruined?" Heather almost screamed. Anna was grateful for the fountain's loud splashing.

"It's not necessary for you to know," said Michel. "I, myself, know."

"Your sister," Anna said. One of his eyelids trembled.

"One must go on," he said after a silence in which he brought the eyelid under control. He turned back to Heather, detached again. "You must go on."

His advice, which infuriated the girl, saddened Anna. He disguised dark depths with charm and narcissism. He must have done great harm for Sebastian to bother engaging with him. Sebastian did not often bother with people.

All of those drinks the man had ferried from his locker and the bar. All that attention to herself.

Heather suddenly spat, regaining the ecstasy of anger. "'One must go on'? 'Refuse to be ruined'? You ruined yourself a long time ago!"

Michel scooted his chair back on the cement pad in an ear-splitting scrape and half-crouched over the table. "You are not the only one to be compromised, Heather!"

Though Anna was silenced by her racing heart, Heather had been set free. Lifting her head and looking Michel in the eye, she aimed insults with a wild mix of contempt and pride. "You have no idea what I went through. You sit in your comfortable retirement, talking about yourself day and night, bragging on your sculpture, your gallery—your *past,* all your supposed accomplishments from the *past*—but you never talk about how evil you are—"

Michel lifted his index finger and reached across the table to shake it near Heather's face. "I've experienced far more evil than you ever have. I know myself. I know myself far better than you know *your*self."

Heather's eyes narrowed. "Dad has so much dirt on you," she shouted, lunging forward in a paroxysm of tattling. At that moment she reminded Anna of a proud, brittle pianist she'd once seen on a concert stage, a young woman wearing a bathing suit and stiletto heels on her way to the grand piano, hair waxed into an absurd point so sharp that it lacerated the air above the keyboard as she began playing Scriabin. A music critic later described it, not as a performance, but an intoxicated *tantrum.*

"Your past is far worse than anyone knows," Heather finished in a blaze of loathing.

Michel lowered himself into his chair. "Your father isn't the first to know," he said. "Nahum already knows." He glanced quickly at Anna and away. "The Oaks knows. They were good enough to expunge the ancient past." Anna watched his breathing slow, the rise and fall of his chest return to normal. Though she couldn't see his face in the dark, she had the impression it had resumed its arch contours. He was very good-looking. Just before erotic interest drained away, she experienced a moment of tenderness.

He pushed his chair back and stepped away from the table. "I'll give you the privacy to talk about me," he said over his shoulder, already distant, self-protective, amused. This gifted man serving drinks to all and sundry, talking, bragging to anyone within hearing distance, was walking away from two women who were going to dish the dirt on him. A lonely widower who, in the end, Anna thought, departs, solitary and contaminated.

Chapter Twenty-One

With darkness hiding their faces, a breeze wafting between them, Anna and Heather almost relaxed.

"Dad can't stand Mike," Heather said.

"When he first met him in the parking lot," said Anna, "he was captivated by the man's conversation."

"Not anymore. He's learned about Mike's past. Sales. Of women."

Selling women? Anna could not square the Michel she knew, the elderly, elegant, talented, frivolous man she liked, with the predator she was hearing about.

"He went to prison for it," Heather said. "Dad looked him up. Not just the internet. He hired a detective, too."

"How long ago did those things happen?"

"Does it matter?" Heather said edgily.

Anna hoped it had been years and years ago. She repressed the wish that Sebastian had not discovered so much about Michel.

"Dad did the right thing," Heather declared into the silence.

"Yes," said Anna. "He did." Perhaps the comfortable family home on Woodland Street, the friends and neighbors protecting her throughout widowhood, had left her slack. Comfortable. Ignorant. Here at The Oaks, a place designed to protect the elderly from danger, her eyes were being opened.

On Woodland Street, she never tipped too far one way or the other. Morally, on Woodland Street, she walked a steady line between expected and doubtful behavior. She was successful, ignorant, and—asleep.

"Dad thought we should know about Michel," Heather insisted. "He thought I should know and Nahum should know, though Nahum already knew. He thought Michel should know that we know." She looked pointedly at Anna. "He definitely wanted you to know."

"He could have just told me privately, without dragging Michel into it. The man has already been punished."

Heather turned her head slightly sideways. "Dad's afraid you've fallen for him."

"For Heaven's sake," Anna said emptily.

When she and Heather went upstairs to her apartment, she noticed, gratified, that Sebastian and Nahum had made coffee and were helping themselves to crackers and cheese. Sebastian knew where everything was.

"We made ourselves at home," said Nahum.

"I'm glad you did."

"It's late, I should be going," he added without stirring from his chair

"Hold on a minute," said Sebastian, putting out a restraining hand that wasn't necessary since Nahum hadn't moved. "Tell Anna."

"Why don't *you* tell her?" said Nahum.

Sebastian and Nahum were the ones dishing the dirt now, Anna thought. She and Heather sat side by side on the sofa.

"Michel went to prison for running a network of what he called art films," said Sebastian. "Among other things."

"We call it pornography," Nahum added.

"And selling women," Sebastian said, smoothing his tangled hair. To Anna it seemed that he had finally rescued his daughter. Though she was happy for him, she suppressed tears. He could make her cry. Michel, too. And Heather. Was there no one for whom she would not shed tears? Her daughter? Her husband? The man she killed?

Nahum looked at his watch. He glanced over the room that had grown quiet. "Good night, Aunt Anna," he said, rising to give her a kiss. Anna followed him to the door and accompanied him to the elevators, then turned back to the living room where Sebastian had already crossed the carpet to sit on the sofa beside his daughter.

Maybe intimacy is finally achieved when it can no longer be held back, she thought, settling into the space Sebastian was making for her.

Chapter Twenty-Two

When the last of the glasses and plates were lined up in their racks, water surging in the dishwasher, Sebastian walked back to the study. "She's not on the internet," he said, returning to the kitchen. Anna felt his relief. The apartment's air conditioning clicked on. A breeze from the kitchen vent lifted fine hairs off the back of her neck as she handed him port in the juice glass he preferred over finer glassware.

She smoothed her hair upward toward her chignon. "Is it too warm outside to open the sliding doors?"

He looked bored; she was talking about the weather. "If you want to open them, go ahead," he said, staring glumly into the port. She decided against it. "Heather wants to move," he said as they stepped to the dining area. "I told her I can rent the space next to us if she needs room to paint." At the table he pulled out a chair for Anna, then one for himself. "Hell, she can *live* there if she wants to. But she doesn't say yes and she doesn't say no."

Maybe she's tired of living in a warehouse basement. Aloud, Anna offered a platitude as they sat down. "She's still recovering from Chicago."

He studied the effect of dwindling daylight on the juice glass. "She doesn't mention going back to Chicago, thank God. But when I ask her where she wants to live, she doesn't have an answer."

"She wants to be near you," Anna suggested.

"The warehouse basement *is* near me," he said sharply. "Couldn't be closer." After a pause, he added, "What makes you say that?"

"She told me so. She's concerned about you, Sebastian."

He returned to the study of his port.

"She thinks you're upset. Not sleeping well at night. Napping during the day. Not producing." Anna had thought Heather was engaging in backward thinking the night she described Sebastian as troubled. Inside-out thinking because it was *Heather* who was troubled.

"Who wouldn't be upset?" he said. "I'll work it out."

When she was young, Anna would have been surprised that a seventy-year-old man still had things *to work out*; that at eighty, she herself would still be *working things out*. A young woman like Heather was bound to experience some confusion and heartbreak. That was to be expected.

Not trafficking, of course. Not rape. But confusion and heartbreak. Still, little Anna, standing between her parents in their church pew, singing with complete confidence in the ultimate outcome a good Methodist child could look forward to, had believed in happy adulthood and old age. Happy endings for herself and for all good people. *We plow the fields and scatter the good seed on the ground.* Planting and reaping. Harvest time.

Sebastian was turning the juice glass around and around on the table cloth. "She has a lot to learn."

"Heather?" Anna said. "Well, yes. We all do."

He emptied the glass and returned it to the kitchen. Straying into the living room, he stood at the windows, gazing out at the mottled sky.

"Is it going to rain?" She was talking about the weather again. Taking a seat in the rocking chair near him, she supported the bowl of her stemmed glass with one hand, wishing the nutty warmth of sherry could quiet the air swirling about Sebastian's height and head of wiry gray hair. His restless weather affected her down here at sea level. She swallowed some sherry. "Do you and Heather want to stay overnight?"

"Ask *her*," said Sebastian. Eventually, though, he walked back to the study and asked her himself. Their voices added a layer of sound over the muffled television.

"She says yes," he reported back. Anna wanted Sebastian himself to say yes. It had been weeks since they'd made love. But these days he seemed to consult Heather before anyone else. Anna didn't recognize the man who no longer consulted himself first.

"I don't hear the TV," he said when they'd migrated to the bedroom. Unfolding clean pajamas from his shelf in the closet, he added, "She usually falls asleep with the TV on. Though I don't know why she should be tired. She doesn't do anything."

"Has she started painting again?"

"No." He climbed into bed.

"Does she see friends?"

"Not that I can tell, unless it's when I'm out." Anna laid her hand on his shoulder. "As far as my sleeping in the afternoon," he said irritably, moving away from her touch, "she exaggerates. I take a cat nap now and then." From the far edge of the bed he added, "I have a lot on my mind, Anna. Be patient with me."

Lying here beside him, his weathered face turned away, her body's stirring kept her awake. But he had no interest in an arched back, lifted breasts and pelvis. She, too, turned away. Eventually they both slept.

When she awoke in the night, he was gone. She went to the living room, passing Heather's closed door on the way. He was sitting in the rocker, saturated in darkness, head to one side, asleep. When she turned on a lamp, he opened his eyes. "I couldn't sleep."

"Your routine is disturbed," she said, sinking into the sofa.

"I'm aware of that," he snapped.

She was startled into full wakefulness. "Heather is right."

"About what?"

"Right to be concerned about you."

"The attention is gratifying," he said, folding his arms, "but the best thing for both of you to do is let me work it out."

Anna leaned forward on the sofa. "When you say *work it out*, what do you mean?"

"Just that. Work it out."

"Talk to me, Sebastian," she persisted in the near-dark. "If not now, soon. I don't know how to—proceed."

"You don't have to *proceed*, Anna. No one is asking you to *proceed*." Outside, tree branches moved in the night breeze, revealing, then obscuring street lights beyond the deep lawn.

"Shall I just forget you and Heather?" Her voice cracked. Heather stumbled out of the study and down the hall.

"Hi, honey," her father said, setting the rocking chair in motion. "Did we wake you?"

Heather looked from her father to Anna and sat down at the far end of the sofa. "What time is it?"

"Three-thirty," said Anna.

Heather slumped against the cushions. "What's the matter?"

"Nothing's the matter," Sebastian said.

"He can't sleep," said Anna.

"Please don't try and explain me to my daughter."

Heather lifted her ragged face and asked again, "What's the matter, Dad?" Sebastian braced his elbows on the arms of the rocking chair, his face vacant with fatigue. The lamp flickered, as if the electric power to the apartment couldn't function on the room's human grid. Heather stood and turned toward the study and pull-out sofa. "I'm going back to bed," she said. "How about you, Dad?"

"Maybe." Hesitating, he pushed himself up out of the rocker and followed his daughter back along the hallway. Amid the closing of doors,

Anna stared into the small circle of lamplight. She'd seldom heard Heather suggest a sensible course of action. And she'd never seen Sebastian in need of direction. Without turning off the lamp, she returned to the bedroom where she lay down, covered herself, and stared out the sliding glass door at a hanging flower pot swaying from the balcony eave. Beside her, Sebastian took controlled, self-conscious breaths in a poor imitation of sleep.

Next morning he was up early making coffee. Still in her robe and slippers, Anna slid into a chair at the dining room table.

"Morning," he said, moving about the kitchen without momentum. There was usually something he wanted to do next; wanted intensely to do next. Charmed, distracted, Anna routinely accepted his forward motion and simply bobbed in his wake. If he pulled away from her, well, she knew how to float—sometimes for days, sometimes for weeks—in the slow current of her less vivid but sufficient daily life. "I recall that I may have been difficult last night," he said. Though stopping short of an apology, he was almost contrite. He brought the coffee pot to the dining area, empty cups hanging by their handles from two fingers. "I couldn't sleep," he added unnecessarily.

Drained, she asked without interest, "What's on your agenda today?"

"Maybe I'll do some work in the studio." He gave a subdued snort. "I don't want Heather to think I'm unproductive." He didn't ask Anna if she had an agenda, perhaps because he knew, even if she had one, it wouldn't interest him enough to talk about. She would read the newspaper. Swim. Eat lunch. Fall asleep over a book. Wait for dinner. Help him cook the dinner. Eat the dinner. Watch a little TV. Go to a fondle-less bed.

"Would you like to see the new exhibit they've hung at the artists' co-op?" he asked with a hint of his old enthusiasm. "Heather wants to go this afternoon."

"I'd love to," said Anna. "Does she have something in the show?"

His face darkened. "She hasn't painted since Chicago."

"Still," Anna said, "it's good to see her interested."

Pointlessly, he stirred his cooling coffee. "She has no idea where she wants to live, Anna."

Anna knew he did not think of the space where he lived as a warehouse basement. *She's lived here most of her life,* he would say. *She loves it. It's her home.*

Heather came to the table in stale Levi's and tee-shirt.

"Coffee?" asked Sebastian. She sat in a foggy silence.

"I'll make toast," said Anna.

Staring at her as if unaware of what she was looking at, Heather said, "How many mornings have you been making toast and coffee, Anna?"

"Well, I started drinking coffee when I was about twenty. So let's say sixty years' worth of mornings."

"Sixty years," Heather mused in blurry acknowledgment. "On Woodland Street?"

"Most of it. I've never thought of it as an accomplishment, though."

"Oh, but it is," Heather said simply.

"How did you sleep?" Sebastian asked his daughter, coming back to the table with the coffee pot.

"You mean after getting up at three-thirty?"

Sebastian looked chastened.

"Apparently we all fell asleep again," said Anna.

"Speak for yourself," said Sebastian.

"Dad! I heard you snoring all the way from my room."

"It was only intermittent sleep," he said. "What time shall we pick up Anna for the exhibit this afternoon?"

"Are we still going?"

"I thought that's what you wanted."

"Maybe."

He looked over at Anna. "We'll let you know."

Anna turned her attention inward and made other plans.

"We'll call you," he said.

"You won't need to."

"How will you know whether we're going or not?"

"It won't matter. I have other plans."

"We'll go," Heather said, her face coloring. "We'll definitely go."

"Whatever you want," Sebastian said.

Anna went to the kitchen. *He means it. Whatever you want, Heather.* "Two o'clock," she heard Heather say decisively.

"Two o'clock," Sebastian repeated as Anna came back with the toast. Though this was just one more toast-and-coffee morning, to Anna it felt different from other mornings. She mattered to Heather.

Chapter Twenty-Three

"I guess the sale of your Woodland Street house is final," Sebastian said several days later, down-shifting for a stop sign. Even though Anna assured him The Oaks van delivered residents to their medical appointments, he'd insisted on driving her himself. "Heather wants me to," he explained, an admission that detracted somewhat from his gallantry. "Of course, I want to, too."

"Yes, the sale of the house is quite final. Closing was months ago. Why do you ask?"

He shifted into first and entered the intersection. "No particular reason."

But after the appointment, instead of returning to The Oaks, he drove in the opposite direction and took the roundabout that emptied into Woodland Street. Anna closed her eyes and endured sudden weakness as the truck swerved around the center whose flowers and grass flourished as if she had not caused a fatal accident here.

Once they turned into Woodland Street, Sebastian covered her hand with his. As they approached her old family home, he slowed. She gave the brick walls and casement windows a cursory glance, not wanting to be heartsick twice on Woodland. He circled the block of turn-of-the-twentieth-century homes and, without a word, returned and parked across the street from 915. Drapes were drawn in the upstairs corner that had been her bedroom as a child and, later, Marianna's nursery. She couldn't see the master bedroom whose wall of windows overlooked the back yard with its cherry trees and spirea bushes rooted in a lawn she now remembered as always green. Gradually, awareness of her parents, husband, daughter, her own years of solitude and recovery in the house, calmed her. She rotated her wrist and lifted her hand in Sebastian's, palm to palm. He turned back from the house and said unexpectedly, "Those were good years."

Some of them were good, Sebastian. She slowed the moving pictures rolling swiftly through her mind: piano practice before school, her mother beside her on the bench listening carefully because she'd always wanted piano lessons herself. Her father taking the stairs two steps at a time to bathe in the claw-footed tub following hospital rounds in the polio ward; he didn't want to infect his wife and daughter. Years later, the utter happiness when Lorenzo agreed to move into 915. The birth of their baby daughter. Picnics in the back yard. The emptiness of the master bedroom and of the nursery after their deaths. Her wails behind the brick walls. Her carelessness in dress, in housekeeping, when she and the house competed to see who, what, could deteriorate faster. The slow return of work and sanity. The new relationship with the man now sitting beside her.

She hadn't known he was fond of Woodland Street. "Do you miss the house?"

But he was already rolling his own moving pictures. "Do you remember the night I came to tell you I'd made arrangements to have a child?"

"How could I forget?"

"I've wondered sometimes why I felt I had to tell you."

"Eventually I would have known."

"I mean why I felt the pressing need to tell you that same night."

"The night you slept with Heather's—mother?"

He looked shocked. "I didn't tell you *then*, Anna," he said. "I told you the night I learned she was pregnant."

She shrugged, almost amused. *What difference would it make if I'd learned a few weeks after you made love with a stranger?*

Now Sebastian was the one with the hint of a smile, as if he'd heard her thoughts, which he probably had; they'd known each other such a long time. "It wasn't love, Anna. It was never love. It wasn't lust, either. It was necessity. I wanted a child."

"I remember it was raining hard that night."

"I remember."

"You hung your umbrella on the door knob."

"*That* I don't remember." Through the truck's windshield the sky was serenely blue, as serene as Woodland Street here below. If a cloud drifted across the sun, it soon floated off to the east, leaving the beds of daffodils and bearded iris as untroubled as before. Sebastian rested his softening hands on the top half of the steering wheel. His arms, too, seemed to be softening. Losing muscle. She wanted to stroke the silky gray hairs, a soft, arousing pelt along his forearm.

"How would things be different if Heather had grown up on Woodland Street?" he was saying.

The question stunned Anna. "If we'd raised her together?"

"I just mean if she'd grown up on Woodland Street."

"Just you and Heather in my Woodland Street house?"

He looked away. "Well, you would have been there, too."

"You're fantasizing about my house without me in it?"

He twisted toward her, his elbow grinding against the steering wheel for leverage, his mouth half open. Anna quashed her sense of not mattering to him. "I don't remember ever hearing you express fondness for the house," she said.

He dropped his arm from the steering wheel. Anna was as conscious of the smells in the cab— oil, gasoline, dust from highways and roads— as she was of his colorless, riveting eyes. "Woodland is not my kind of street," he said

"You spent countless days and nights on this street, Sebastian."

"I admit to enjoying its comforts."

"You're thinking my house would have been a good place to raise Heather?"

"Possibly. It's a conventional house. She might have liked that." He ran a finger around the sagging sun visor. "But she wasn't brought up to be conventional." The blue sky, in addition to being pleasant, now took on orderly, protective qualities. Short of a tornado, flood, or earthquake, 915 Woodland would sit on its green, green lawn, forever dimpled, forever conventional. "I'll admit I was comfortable here," he repeated. "Still, the studio is my world."

"The studio suits you," she said. "You were never looking for comfort or safety."

"The studio isn't *un*safe, Anna, though I'll admit it's not as comfortable as it might be." He dropped one hand onto the knob of the stick shift. "Maybe it hasn't been quite right for Heather."

Possibly, Sebastian.

"She likes The Oaks."

"Conventional," said Anna.

"I know. But she likes it."

"With or without me in it?"

"With you in it."

"I give you credit, Sebastian. Growing up in your studio, she's developed into an interesting person. And an artist."

He re-centered himself at the steering wheel. "She might have always grown up that way, even on Woodland Street."

The run of concessions dried up. "In my house."

He folded his arms and leaned against the steering wheel. "Do you think we could have raised her together?"

"I doubt it. You didn't want my help."

"How can you say that, Anna?"

"You never noticed that I would have liked to be closer to her?"

He shrugged and fiddled with the key in the ignition. "That would have been up to Heather, wouldn't it?"

Glancing back at the house, she saw herself as a cipher. Just one more person in a world so populous that we say *people* instead of *persons*. "Comfort and convenience aside, Sebastian, was I ever important to you?"

"I'm here, aren't I?" he said. "I followed you to The Oaks. It's not my kind of place, but—"

"Am I your kind of person, Sebastian?"

"Yes," he said. "You always have been." He looked annoyed. "I'm surprised I have to tell you." She was somewhat mollified. "Would it be possible for you to buy the house again?" he said casually. The question was like a thunder clap. Her thoughts shot forward in a spasm of disbelief.

"Buy it back?"

"Yes. Buy it back."

"But I'm living in The Oaks now."

"It was just a passing thought." But she knew it wasn't a passing thought.

"Heather's grown," she said. "We can't go back in time, Sebastian."

He turned the key in the ignition, stomped on the clutch, and peeled out of Woodland Street. Anna braced herself against the dashboard. He drove too fast around the roundabout, the roundabout she had entered timidly just before—killing a man. Flooded with sudden rage, she flung out accusations. "For years you were happy enough to spend nights in my house! To cook in a kitchen larger than a galley! To have your underwear and pajamas washed and folded and laid neatly on your special shelf!" She was almost screaming above the rough old engine.

Breathing heavily, he delivered her to The Oaks. "I'm offended," he said, stopping the truck and barely waiting for her to step down onto the pavement.

How satisfying the metal shriek of the door as she slammed it behind her. How empty the circular drive when he left and turned toward town. Inside, she passed several residents on the way to the elevator without noticing who they were.

Chapter Twenty-Four

"Can we come for dinner tonight?" Heather's voice sounded child-like. The two of them almost never spoke on the telephone.

"Of course," said Anna, surprised. She hadn't seen Sebastian since they'd quarreled a week earlier.

"We'll pick up some groceries on the way over."

"I need milk and eggs."

"Are you making bread pudding with raisins?"

"Indeed I am." An hour later when the doorbell rang, Heather was alone. "Where's your dad?"

Heather carried the groceries into the kitchen. "He had other plans." She set the bag on the counter and unpacked the food.

"We'll have a nice dinner, just the two of us," Anna said. But when Heather left for the living room, the silence in the apartment was more the sound of Heather minus her father than true silence. When dinner was on the table, she called Heather and they sat across from each other, eating politely, cutting their chicken with precision.

"I enjoyed the art exhibit last week," Anna said. "The community center is a good venue."

"Dad thought the paintings were mediocre."

"Well, we all do the best we can," Anna said lamely.

"He wants me to start painting again," Heather said.

"And you?"

Heather looked up. "And me what?"

"Do you want to paint?"

"Well, yeah." They continued cutting, chewing, swallowing. "There isn't room in the studio."

"Is there some other space you could use?"

Heather played with her food. "What's in The Oaks basement?"

Anna hid her astonishment by wiping her mouth with her napkin. "Heating and cooling, I think. I've only been down there once or twice. Storage space. The residents are assigned locked stalls for their extra belongings. Cages, really."

"Can you show me sometime?"

"Sure. After dinner, if you like."

When Heather remained silent, Anna said, "Are you and your dad thinking of storing work down there? I have some space in my stall."

Heather looked out the window and back to the table. "I was wondering about renting space to live in."

Anna stared. "The Oaks basement?"

Heather didn't answer.

"You want to live at The Oaks?"

"Just a thought," Heather said, red coloration climbing from her throat.

"It's an interesting thought," Anna said. "We can take a minute after dinner and look around."

Heather didn't say yes or no.

"I own my apartment," Anna said illogically. "Just the apartment."

"I guess there's an age limit for residents here," Heather said.

"Fifty-five."

"I guess no one lives in the basement."

"No one lives in the basement." Anna cleared the table and brought in the bread pudding. "Your dad's eligible for The Oaks," she said, "if he's interested." She went back for dessert bowls.

"I wasn't thinking of Dad," Heather said. They ate the pudding without enjoyment.

"What other possible locations are you considering?"

Heather let her spoon rest in the bowl and leaned back against the straight chair. "Different ideas occur to me at different times," she said. "I was wondering if I could trade work for living at The Oaks."

"Like..."

"Like cleaning apartments or working in the kitchen. Maybe waiting tables in the dining room." She brightened. "Or maybe helping residents with things they need, like shopping or running errands. Driving. Helping people with the internet."

"The internet comes with problems," Anna couldn't help saying.

"Not everyone on the internet is dangerous," Heather said defensively.

Or a felon. "Of course not, Heather."

"I can take care of myself now." She leaned forward. "That's why I want to move. Because I can take care of myself."

"Of course you can."

"That's why I'm asking about The Oaks. Dad doesn't think I can take care of myself."

But The Oaks is for old people who can't take care of themselves, Heather. Anna's thinking underwent an almost physical adjustment as she tried to comprehend the young woman seated across from her. She knew how to go through the motions of listening; refraining from judgement; refraining from comment. But she must do more. Wrench herself from stupefaction. Take on Heather's feelings. Experience betrayal. Violation. Rape. She must become a young woman who needs to regain herself and doesn't know how.

"The Oaks has a security system, doesn't it?" Heather asked.

"The doors are locked every night at eight-thirty and Security works till seven the next morning," Anna answered, sincere. Factual.

Heather's eyes narrowed at the change she sensed. "Are you making fun of me?"

"Not at all. I'm imagining how you feel. Tell me if I'm wrong." She went back to her pudding. Heather, watching her closely, did not tell her she was wrong.

After the dishes were done, the two of them went down to the basement. The elevator doors slid open onto half light provided by low-watt bulbs hanging just above locked cages. "It smells kind of damp down here," Heather said.

"Damp cement," said Anna, noticing drains sunk at regular intervals into the slab floor.

"Where's your storage?"

Anna led Heather between rows toward a back corner. "Somewhere back here," she said.

"I guess they're all locked."

"They're all locked." She found her stall and twirled the wheel of the combination lock. "I may not have the numbers right," she said, trying a second time.

Peering between uprights at packing boxes, chairs piled upside-down on a table, Heather said, "Did you get rid of a lot of stuff when you moved?"

Anna was still fiddling with the lock. "Yes. Before The Oaks, I lived in a nine-room house."

"I remember the house," Heather said. "Brick."

"It was in my family for years."

"I was there a few times when I was little."

"I remember your visits well." Anna gave up on the lock. "At least you see what it's like down here."

"It looks sturdy," Heather said, studying the uprights of the stall. "The basement wouldn't work for painting, though. Too dark. But it *is* safe." They returned to the elevator that stood open as if waiting for them. "The doors don't close automatically?" she asked.

"Not this time, I guess." Anna pushed the button for the fifth floor.

"Doors shouldn't just stand open," Heather scolded. "There's a lot of crime everywhere. Did you know an old woman was attacked in her house a few months ago? Right here in town? Did you read about it? She was watching TV and a man got into a back bedroom. She didn't hear him break the window. They're still looking for the serial killer in St. Louis who raped and murdered another woman who was also living alone. And he broke a window in a back bedroom, too. The M.O. is the same. No place is safe, Anna. Don't kid yourself. The Oaks is not as safe as you think it is."

By this time they'd reached the fifth floor and were stepping off the elevator. Anna had not locked her apartment.

"You should lock your apartment, Anna. Anyone could walk in."

"They would have to pass the front desk first."

"Dad and I have passed the front desk more than once when no one was there," Heather said. "Do you mind checking the back rooms and all the closets?"

Instead, Anna took Heather by both hands and drew her to the sofa. Gone was the empathy she'd felt earlier, the sensitive perception of Heather's fear. "I moved to The Oaks because I was afraid of living alone in my house," she said firmly. "I wasn't afraid of crime, but I was afraid of falling or having an attack of some kind. I was afraid of dying alone." She withdrew her hands from Heather's. "I was afraid of dying."

Heather moved to the middle of the sofa and looked away. "You could die *here*, Anna. In your apartment."

"That's just the point," said Anna. "There's no such thing as perfect safety."

"You could be murdered by an intruder," Heather warned, not even hearing. "The Oaks isn't as safe as it looks. Especially when you don't lock your door."

"Nothing is perfectly safe—" Anna started to repeat.

"And what about the people who clean the apartments? The hallways?" Heather's face was animated by disaster. "Repairmen? Electricians? Nothing is safe. Not even The Oaks."

"Of course it isn't," agreed Anna.

"Why didn't you stay in your house?" Heather's face cleared in a spasm of trust. "Dad would have helped you."

"He *did* help me," Anna said. "He was wonderful. He didn't like leaving you alone at night, but—"

"He left me alone at night?"

"Just until I was able to take care of myself. Go to the bathroom alone."

"How could he leave me alone?"

"Only when you were asleep."

"But that's exactly when people attack!"

Anna laid her arm along the back of the sofa. "Heather, were you asleep when you were attacked in Chicago?"

Heather's face swung closed, like a gate on a tight spring that prevents entry.

"I can't imagine the terror," Anna said.

Hiding her face with her hands, Heather cried, "You should try!" When she dropped her hands, her face was wet and mottled. "If you knew, you wouldn't leave your apartment unlocked!"

After a time, with Heather's inflamed face beginning to compose itself, Anna said, "Let's go outside, Heather. There's a small garden—"

Heather looked out the window. "It's almost dark."

"We'll make sure we're back before nightfall," Anna said. She smiled a little. "And we'll lock the door behind us."

"You bet we will." Apparently humoring the older woman, Heather followed her to the hallway where, with sharp oversight, she watched the key being turned in the lock. Moments later, they reached the main floor. In the lounge, faint light, pink residue from the sunset, filtered through Venetian blinds. Heather cast a backward glance at the closing elevator doors.

"Did you see the woman behind the front desk?" Anna asked as they stepped outside. "Someone is always there."

Heather sniffed, doubtful. They walked along the sidewalk leading around the front wing of the building. Under the darkening sky, the back lawn looked gray. With recent irrigation from the automated water system, it smelled less like pampered grass than wet dirt.

"Where's the garden?" Heather asked.

"A little farther." When they reached the oak trees and clumps of columbine not yet in bloom, Anna sat down on a wooden bench punctuated by a brass plaque, illegible in twilight. Heather perched on the edge. Nestled in clay pots, geranium seedlings promised splashes of color all the way to the back property line. A gravel path curved off toward the grove of oaks, already shadowy.

"Do you come out here alone?" Heather asked.

"Yes, though I'm seldom alone. Other residents come to the garden. And there are always maintenance people around. Women maintenance people, too," she said pointedly.

"I can't wait to get old," Heather said impulsively.

"My goodness," said Anna, amusement coloring her surprise. "Most people say they wish they were young again."

"Well, do *you* wish you were young again?"

Anna gazed over at the oaks, overlords of vanished prairie, pasture land, farmstead, and now, manicured property. "The trees," she said, "have escaped drought, fire, lightning, lumber sales, real estate interests."

"They're at peace," Heather said.

"There's a lot of sentimentality about old age," said Anna. "And a lot of phony memories about being young." Heather seemed to have forgotten it was dark.

"You've got your life behind you," she said. "You know how everything turned out."

Anna threw back her head and laughed out loud. "I don't have the faintest idea how everything turned out. Or how things are *going* to turn out." Heather looked sheepish. "For instance, I don't know where you're going to paint. Or where you're going to live. I don't know whether your dad will talk to me again."

"He will."

"His experience of Chicago has thrown him off-course."

"It's *my* experience," Heather objected. "Not Dad's."

"Yes," said Anna, "but it's upset him. He won't talk about it."

"He'll work it out," Heather said. "He'll start making pottery again. He talks about doing some drawing."

"Is that what he says?"

"Yeah. He'll start to feel better. You'll see." Heather's words seemed automatic to Anna: a script. She imagined father and daughter together in a house surrounded by fencing, hedges, one of them painting in one room, the other working a potter's wheel in another. This house in her imagination seemed as strange as the warehouse basement. She admitted to herself that Sebastian's studio had never conformed to her idea of a suitable place to live or raise a child. Nor was it suitable for a father to go looking for his child's mother; a woman to impregnate. His way of life, she'd always told herself, was a sign of his originality; his creativity. Nevertheless, Sebastian had always seemed border-line strange to her. Even if he moved into a structure with rooms and doors and windows, his presence would imprint any house with oddity.

She had always thought him odd. Perhaps he'd always known this. Perhaps that was why he'd never shared his daughter with her.

She had mistakenly expected the garden to be restful for both Heather and herself. "Let's go back inside," she said. "Why don't you spend the night here with me. We'll talk. I'll tell you about old age and you can tell me about being young." She led the way back from the garden to the sidewalk running alonside the lawn and around to the entrance, refraining, in the lobby, from pointing out that the elevator doors were safely closed. The two of them shot up to the fifth floor, but before she could unlock the door to her apartment, her neighbor came out to meet them in a bathrobe. "Anna," Meg said, her eyes wide, "I just heard some sad news. Michel is in the hospital." Anna held her key in midair. She thought of the man's handsome head and tailored suits. She thought of his sister.

"What happened?"

"He had a heart attack." Meg was ready to elaborate, but Anna interrupted her. "Thank you for telling me."

"It's such a shock when an ambulance comes for one of us..."

Anna and Heather went into the apartment. Heather bolted the door. "Michel is the artist from Miami, right? Mike."

Anna nodded. Neither of them spoke about the man's criminal past. Nothing about the night Heather had screamed at him on The Oaks sunporch. It was the first time Anna had seen Heather furious about the sex crimes against her. Wherever he was, Michel whipped up interest. Around him, things came alive, for good or bad.

"He has a presence," Anna said, and realized how much she had once liked him. "The night clothes you left here last time are on a shelf in the den closet." She was storing clothing for Heather, laundering it, folding it, just as she'd done for Sebastian over the years. How had this happened? When she was a young woman, she'd thought her future was settled: wife and mother. Later there would be a professional career. But it turned out, instead of creating a family with Lorenzo and Marianna, she'd taught law and, on the side, half-wifed Sebastian. Now she was half-mothering Heather, a girl who wanted to be an old woman living in The Oaks.

"I'll trade you places," she said a little later when they'd settled at the table with tea and a soft drink. "You can be an old woman living in The Oaks and I'll be eighteen."

But Heather had sunk into moroseness and was not amused. "I don't know how to be eighty, and I don't know how to be eighteen," she said. She looked at Anna with envy. "You've done both."

"It's not something I accomplished on my own," Anna said. "Really, I didn't notice it was happening." Heather sat, letting the ice in her soda melt. "I was fortunate, Heather. The boys and men I knew were courteous. I never experienced violence from a man. Or anyone."

"Dad says you've lived a safe life."

Anna lifted her chin in defiance. "He didn't know my husband."

"He knows he was Black."

"It wasn't a safe marriage for either of us."

"But he didn't rape you or lock you up and feed you drugs."

"In that sense it was safe." Anna made herself into a receptacle for listening. Consciously hoisting herself above the conformity Sebastian accused her of, she reflected back to Heather neither sympathy nor moral judgement. But Heather was providing the moral judgement herself.

"Anyone else would have known he wasn't an art dealer," she said, not bothering to name the ever-present man stalking her thoughts.

"The internet catches many people unaware," Anna said.

"Not the smart ones." Heather pushed her drink away and adjusted her position, struggling against the chair rather than settling into it.

"You and your dad haven't followed usual paths, Heather. You've been isolated in a warehouse basement."

"Not paths, Anna. Path. Dad's path. And it's not my warehouse apartment. It's Dad's."

"Well," Anna began—

"—and now he doesn't trust his path."

Anna was surprised at the insight. *I don't think I ever trusted his path, either, Heather.*

"If I move out," the girl was saying, "it will be somewhere near so I can visit often. He needs me."

"Yes, he does."

"He needs you, too," Heather said. "You can help him."

"I don't think he wants my help."

"Not right now," Heather agreed. "But eventually he will need you again."

"I'm ten years older than he is, Heather. *Eventually* is a questionable concept."

"You're in good health," Heather insisted.

"Perhaps. For now. There's my high blood pressure. My prolapsed vagina."

"What's a prolapsed vagina?"

"When tissue protrudes outside of the vagina. When the vagina doesn't hold the bladder up where it belongs. From childbirth, I suppose. Uteruses and vaginas receive quite a battering."

Heather cringed.

"You've already experienced battering. Force."

"Will I have a prolapsed vagina?" Heather whispered.

"Perhaps you will. But you'll be able to live with it. I do."

Heather frowned. "Old women are inside-out."

"They can be."

"I don't think Dad knows about this stuff."

"Men prefer not to know."

Heather sat silent. "Dad told me you had a little girl."

"Marianna."

Heather folded her arms and bent forward until her forehead almost touched the tabletop. "I'll never have a child because I'll never have sex. Anyway, I'll barely be able to take care of myself. I can't take care of anyone else." She bent lower until her forehead did actually touch the table. "I can never go through adulthood."

"I think you can, Heather. When the time comes, you'll be able to." She went to the kitchen for ice and added it to Heather's tepid glass. "I would have given anything to care for Marianna."

Heather was still hugging her midriff. "How old would she be now?"

"Older than you."

"Did Dad know her?"

Anna shook her head. "He and I met long after she died."

"What did she die of?"

Anna hesitated. "A car hit her when she ran out into the street."

"Wasn't anyone watching her?"

"I'm afraid not."

After another long silence Heather said, "You could have been my mother." Her eyes wandered about the room until her blank gaze settled on the ceiling.

"I couldn't have," Anna said. "I was already old when you were born."

"Yeah," Heather said without inflection; without any light in her eyes. "Dad wanted a child and so he went out and found a woman who could get pregnant."

"That's what happened. He's being straightforward with you, Heather. He wanted a child. He wanted *you*."

"You could have raised me together."

"Your father and I couldn't be happy living in the same place. I wouldn't want to live in a basement studio and he wouldn't want to live on Woodland Street. We couldn't have raised you together."

Heather's face sharpened. "Did you *have* to live on Woodland Street?"

"It was my family home! My grandparents bought that house."

"So you had to live there?"

"Well—yes."

"Did your husband want to live there?'

"Not at first."

"Dad wouldn't want to live there, that's for sure."

"He wants to now," Anna almost snapped.

"He thinks you belong in your own home, not at The Oaks. He says you're not ready to be in The Oaks."

"Your dad is confused. Regardless of what he says, I belong in The Oaks."

"It's my fault that Dad's confused."

"You didn't choose to be locked up and sold, Heather."

"No, but I believed, you know—him when he said he owned a gallery. I believed he liked my art. And me."

"Your experience is your own," Anna said. "Your recovery is your own." Her voice thickened with a kind of joy. "Your father will come to understand that your life is your own. Your failures are your own, and so are your accomplishments."

Heather looked tired. "I don't have any accomplishments," she said.

Chapter Twenty-Five

"I gather my daughter has been talking to you about her plans," Sebastian said to Anna as they sat across the table from each other at Bob's, a restaurant as plain and reliable as its name, though the recent addition of the word *Bistro* suggested an attempt to update itself.

"She hasn't formulated any plans yet," said Anna.

"*Formulated?*" Sebastian retorted. "That's a word for something Heather doesn't know how to do."

"That will change." They gave their orders to the waiter and hunkered down to nurture their differences. Speaking in modulated tones, yet alternately on the offense, defense, they devoted themselves to Heather.

"She needs to go to school or get a job," Sebastian stated. "She can't just stay at home doing nothing. And she spends too much time at The Oaks." He paused, opinion swerving into outright curiosity. "What does she do when she's at The Oaks?"

"We talk," Anna said, feeling rebuked.

"What do you talk about?"

"Life. Recovering from bad experiences."

"What do you tell her?"

"How I recovered from my child's death and my husband's suicide." He stared. "She needs to *do* something, not just talk."

"She doesn't need to spend so much time with old people," Anna agreed. "She's hiding."

"Not when she's with me," Sebastian said, bristling. "I'm not old."

"Oh yes you are, Sebastian." As they sat in a disagreeable silence, waiting for their food, something unbidden began to overtake Anna. When she looked at Sebastian, it was as if she watched him through a lens that hadn't been properly ground. The tables in the restaurant, the walls, the bar along one side of the room, all seemed smaller than they actually were, and farther away.

Was she undergoing some kind of seizure? Was she an eighty-year-old woman having a stroke? One thought goose-stepped through her mind: she didn't need to sit here and talk to Sebastian about his daughter. She didn't need to welcome Heather into her home every day. For years it had been her preoccupation to offer herself to them.

"What are you thinking?" Sebastian asked. Her plate of food sat untouched. How long had it been sitting here in front of her? "Anna?"

"I'm not thinking much of anything," she prevaricated, picking up her knife and fork. But she dropped them with a clatter. "Sebastian, I don't know why we're sitting here talking about Heather."

"Because she needs help."

"Perhaps she needs yours. She doesn't need mine. And you're right. She's spending too much time at The Oaks."

He looked shocked. "So what are you saying?"

"I'm saying Heather is your daughter." She half-rose. "I'm spending too much time with both of you." She bent and picked up the napkin that had fallen from her lap. "Excuse me." In the bathroom she splashed cool water on her face and made lingering eye contact in the mirror. Though her hands trembled, she did not think she was ill. She was simply excited. Alarmed. She felt herself withdrawing from the life she knew. Except for her hot face and dry lips—a spike in blood pressure—there was no sign of change. But this time she was listening to her blood's advice.

When she returned to the table, Sebastian was eating methodically. Anna tasted a little of her entree and salad before laying down the fork. Sebastian followed by crossing his silverware on his plate and looking at her, eyes steady but foreign, hair wirier than before, a fleck of food in one corner of his mouth. "What's the point of finishing the meal?" he said, and stood.

"I'll pay," said Anna, already turning toward the cash register by the door.

"No, I will." He laid a tip on the table. Outside, they faced each other on the sidewalk.

"Heather's welcome to visit," Anna said, relenting a little.

"I'm not?"

"You don't like The Oaks."

"Don't tell me what I like and don't like, Anna." They walked a half block to the parked truck. It occurred to her she would no longer hear the screech of metal on metal or see his profile behind the wheel. The realization registered, not as regret, but as fact. The ride back to The Oaks felt like the final act in a play. The Oaks, itself, felt like a theatre set. Oddly, she wasn't sad. At the moment, she calmly waited for the ending. An ending she had set in motion. She'd left Woodland Street. She was leaving Sebastian. Perhaps she was not approaching her own end by choice but by being born. She had been dying all along.

Her face was cooler now. The blood pressure spike had subsided. They'd reached The Oaks entrance. "Good-bye," she said, opening the truck door and stepping down onto the pavement. For a moment after she closed the door, Sebastian waited. Then he followed the circular drive and left The Oaks. His pickup joined traffic and was soon indistinguishable from all the other cars and trucks moving forward, carrying him away from Anna, toward something. What it was, was no longer her business.

Chapter Twenty-Six

Nahum was sitting behind the front desk when Anna entered the lobby. She paused, surprised.

"We had a staffing problem," he said, rising and leaning over the counter to catch her hands in his. "I haven't seen you in a while, Aunt Anna."

She searched his face for signs of well-being at the same time she felt herself untethered from Sebastian and Heather. "Are you eating dinner in the dining room, Nahum?"

"That depends on whether you are or not."

"Yes. Yes, I am." Unbelievably, she felt hungry. But when she sat down at a table for two, she'd lost her appetite again. Someone from across the dining room waved to her; she wasn't sure who it was, but she waved back. The peace she'd felt in the first moments of release from Sebastian and Heather disappeared and a sense of strangeness reoccurred. It was as if she were eating in The Oaks dining room for the first time. Someone took her order, an unhealthful choice of appetizer, dessert, and coffee. After several minutes, someone set food down in front of her. She ate. By the time Nahum arrived, she was taking a last bite of dessert.

"Sebastian's not eating with you tonight?"

"Not ever again," she said. "Sebastian and Heather are on their own, Nahum. I've left him." He almost ducked as if to avoid a missile. "They have to figure things out for themselves. Ever since Heather came back from Chicago, the two of them have been leaning on me. They don't have their feet under them."

He sat down across from her. "Both of them?"

"All four, Nahum. All four feet. Sebastian wants to live in the past. He asked me if I could buy back the house on Woodland Street. And Heather wants to live in The Oaks."

Nahum was busy fielding Anna's words. "Your old house?" He'd spent hours and hours on Woodland Street with Anna and Lorenzo, he reminded her. "I loved Woodland Street." His eyes wandered from his aunt's face. "Are you going to buy it back?" He sounded almost hopeful.

"Certainly not!" Who were these people who cared more about Woodland Street than about her?

Nahum refocused. "Heather is too young to live in The Oaks."

"That's obvious," Anna said crisply. She watched his thoughts—doubt, sympathy—criss-cross his face. "I can't be their wife and mother, Nahum. I never have been and I can't start now." He was not understanding her position, this nephew with whom she'd always shared a bond of family closeness.

"These dilemmas are never easy," he said without conviction.

"It's not a dilemma! It's a simple choice! Either they develop some independence, or—"

"Are they asking to live with you, Aunt Anna?"

"I think they are, Nahum. One wants to live on Woodland Street and the other wants to live at The Oaks. Both places are home to *me*, not to *them*."

"Do they really want to leave their apartment?"

"It's not an apartment, Nahum. It's a dank little studio in the basement of a warehouse."

"But it's theirs."

"It's his. Heather lives there because her father lives there." Anna clutched her linen napkin. "And now she's afraid to move out."

"Heather and Sebastian aren't going to bounce back from her assault"—he snapped his fingers—"just like that. And," he added meaningfully, "neither are you." When she recovered from a dry sob, he continued, "Is Sebastian in free fall?"

"You mean a downward spiral? Yes, I think so."

He leaned back, reflective. "It'll take time. I was in free fall when The Oaks tried to fire me this spring."

"The Oaks was terribly wrong about you," said Anna. "But in Sebastian's case, there's no one to blame."

"Well, crime. His daughter's trafficker."

"Yes," Anna nearly cut him off, "but if Sebastian had raised her sensibly—"

"He must feel that he never accomplished anything after all."

"What did he accomplish?"

"He raised a child."

Anna sat back. "On his own," she said bitterly.

"That's the point, isn't it?" said Nahum. He smiled slightly. "Hands off, Mother. I can do it myself."

"How selfish," Anna whispered. Someone approached the table to speak with Nahum. She waited, hungry for his time.

When he was free again, his calm gaze encompassed the dining room. "I like this job, you know."

"I'm here because you're here, Nahum." Self-interest began to feel inescapable. "I guess I'm leaning on you."

He smiled. But the next time he looked around the room, his glance had narrowed. "Vicki's brother has tested me. He's tested Vicki even more." His lips and eyes softened. "Vicki and I came close, didn't we."

"Close to what?"

"Being respected." He seemed almost amused at himself, even making soft sounds that come from the chest rather than the throat.

"This business with her brother will all be forgotten, Nahum."

He shook his head doubtfully. "Some family members don't talk to us anymore."

"Who?"

"Distant relatives you probably never met."

"I thought I'd met all of Lorenzo's family at one time or another."

"I doubt it. Some didn't want to meet you."

"Because I was a professor?"

"Maybe."

"Because I'm White?"

"Possibly. Some people," he added after a little silence, "don't want change, even when they say they do."

An hour ago Anna had separated from Sebastian. Already she thought it might be a change she didn't want. Already she was noticing that, in his absence, she loved him.

After Nahum left, she pushed back her chair and got to her feet. Joining the flow of residents toward the elevators, she contemplated the evening ahead: a book. Late-night news. Sleep. Dreams. The return of day. Night again. Without Sebastian.

Chapter Twenty-Seven

"Where's the boyfriend?" Philip asked Anna as he and his wife stepped into the elevator the next morning.

"Doing his thing," Meg answered, substituting her own breezy commentary for Anna's more restrained style. "Anyway, it's none of our business, Phil."

Anna had never called Sebastian her boyfriend. *Boyfriend* trivialized the way she felt about him. To her, he was more a husband than boyfriend. Not a legal husband, but the man in her life who lasted. She'd felt like the wife of an interesting husband who does not control her.

"To me, he's simply Sebastian," she replied.

"Just asking," Philip said, slipping out from under his wife's scolding.

"Anna!" In the dining room, Georgina, wearing an orange pantsuit and large earrings, called out to Anna from the breakfast line. Orville waved. Taking their trays to a table near the window, sunlight bouncing off the pantsuit until it seemed Georgina, herself, might burst into flame, they waited for Anna to join them.

"We haven't seen you in the dining room for weeks," said Orville. Anna smiled and sat down opposite them. Now that she was rejoining community life at The Oaks, her days and nights would be unvarying. Meals in the dining room. Books in the library. Exercise in the exercise room. The Oaks van would drive her shopping and to medical appointments. Sebastian would not call her and she would not call Sebastian.

"Care to join us for a swim one of these days?" Georgina asked, laying down her butter knife and shedding muffin crumbs frontally. She unfurled her cloth napkin.

"The Sharks?"

White linen snapped once above the retaining wall of bosom. "Sure. Or for a free swim. I swim for fun, too, you know. Not just competitively."

Anna pictured Georgina and The Sharks competing against other earnest seniors. Heard whistle shrieks from aging, skinny-shanked swim coaches bouncing off cement and tiles; splashes of chlorinated, blue-green water lathing jellied flesh; thumps of diving boards catapulting Sharks, Porpoises, and Whales into Olympic-sized pools up and down the state.

"Let's swim for fun," said Anna. When was the last time she'd done something because it was fun? "I'll look forward to it." When Orville left for his post-breakfast nap, the two women lingered at their table. Around them, servers shook out fresh tablecloths and laid place settings.

"So how are you? Do you miss Sebastian?" Apparently, gossip still ricocheted off every wall, ceiling, and floor of The Oaks; otherwise, how would Georgina know she was no longer seeing Sebastian? She studied Georgina's face for unkindness. A breach of good manners. A suggestion of pity. Worse, secret pleasure in a friend's disrupted life. But the broad, affable face held nothing more than moderate affection. The only immoderate thing about Georgina was her pantsuit.

"Yes, I guess I do miss him. We've been together for years."

"You haven't talked to him lately?"

"If you mean since yesterday, no."

"Do you think he'll call?"

"How should I know?" Georgina didn't seem offended by Anna's sharp tone. "I mean, I've never known what to expect from him in the past, so why should I now? I certainly don't plan to call *him*."

"How is his daughter?"

"Recovering."

"Orville and I had some terrible fights over our daughter," Georgina said. When the dining room began to clear, they crossed to the reception area. "Those were hard years."

"At least you raised her together."

Georgina cocked her head. "Actually, she's Orville's child."

"I hadn't realized that," Anna said. "When you talk about her, she seems so—yours. Yours together." They stepped into the elevator. When the doors opened again, they were on Anna's floor. "Do you want to come in, Georgina?"

Seeing the window seat at the end of the hall, Georgina said, "Let's sit out here for a minute." The window was graying with a change in weather, cooling the pantsuit's fiery orange. A few drops of rain tapped at the glass.

"How old was Orville's daughter when the two of you married?"

"Twelve." Georgina took one end of the seat. "She didn't like me. She wouldn't have liked any woman her father married."

"Heather never exactly disliked me," Anna said, also sitting. "She just didn't notice me. Until recently."

"How old was she when you met Sebastian?"

"She wasn't born until long after we met."

Georgina stared. "Was Sebastian married before?"

"No. He paid a young woman to carry his daughter and give birth to her."

Georgina's eyes widened. Rain broke free and cascaded down the window. "Who's the mother?"

"I don't know," said Anna.

"Why didn't Sebastian ask *you* to be the mother?"

"I was too old," Anna said simply, her gaze rising to meet Georgina's astonishment. "I'd already gone through menopause." She caught herself smiling an idiotic smile. "I didn't have any more eggs."

If Georgina had not been seated, Anna thought, she would be standing with arms akimbo, fists jammed against orange, outraged, quivering hips.

"He had his reasons," Anna said, resetting her face to unidiotic.

"What reasons could there possibly be?"

"Sebastian is always thinking uncommon thoughts," Anna said. "He's inventive, Georgina. Creative."

"Why didn't he create a marriage?"

"You mean with me?"

"With anyone! To give Heather a mother!"

"If he could have, he would have." Anna found herself defending Sebastian who seemed to be hovering a few steps away at her apartment door. The rip and tear of love that shot through her was shocking. She loved him when he was absent. She covered her face with her hands and wept. Georgina probably thought she was crying because she wasn't Heather's mother; crying because she and Sebastian had never married.

Chapter Twenty-Eight

"How are you, Anna?" Heather said. They hadn't spoken in person or on the telephone for weeks. "Can we have lunch sometime?"

"Of course," Anna said. "I've missed you. Come over and I'll fix us something."

"No, I'll pick you up. Can you be ready by eleven?"

Oh, thought Anna, *you have a car.* Or perhaps she was driving the truck. Since high school, Heather had known how to drive the pickup. "You mean eleven o'clock today?"

"Yes. Today."

Two hours later Heather drove up to The Oaks in an aging Plymouth and stepped out to open the passenger door for Anna.

"Well," said Anna, "this is interesting. I don't think you and I have ever ridden together in a vehicle that wasn't your dad's pickup."

"Nice, isn't it," said Heather, closing the door. Anna leaned on an arm rest patched with duct tape, and waited for Heather to return to the driver's side. "Dad bought it for me." She moved forward along the circular entrance and eased into traffic.

Anna settled back against the worn plush. "Do you miss shifting gears?"

"Kind of. The car is almost too easy to drive." Her hands on the steering wheel were strong and competent. Satisfied. "Have you ever eaten at Duck's Café, Anna? It's a few miles out of town."

"Indeed I have."

"I haven't been there in a long time," Heather said, glancing sideways at Anna and adding casually, "It's been weeks since I've been anywhere near town."

Not only was Anna curious; she felt obligated to inquire. "Why haven't you been anywhere near town, Heather?"

"I've moved."

"Moved?"

"Moved!" Heather reddened with excitement.

"Where?"

"To St. Margaret."

"Where's your dad?"

"In St. Margaret."

Anna sat in stunned silence. "So you're both living in St. Margaret?"

"Yes! I'm a student at The Studios and Dad is a teacher!" She was still red, and blurting. As if set free by the sign at the side of the road—*County Highway B, St. Margaret, 20 Miles*—Heather threw herself into an admission; a shared secret. "I'm taking a studio class in painting, and internet courses in art history and general math!"

"Art history and general math," Anna repeated. "And what is your father doing?"

"Teaching pottery and welding."

Anna sat, ruminative, as thick-leaved hickory and maple glided by.

"Faculty live in a renovated barn and students live in the farmhouse," Heather elaborated.

Anna sat silent. "A barn? A farmhouse?"

Heather laughed. "We'd better get some food in you. You seem stunned."

"I can hardly grasp what you're saying."

Heather was exceeding speed limits, just as her rapid speech exceeded the limits of Anna's comprehension. Sebastian had gotten a job, it seemed, teaching in St. Margaret at The Studios, an arts and vocations school on twenty acres where students and teachers, Heather explained, worked a large vegetable garden, raised chickens, and milked a few cows. She tossed back her head. "I get college credit from Center State College. Dad's known about The Studios for years, but I'm the one who suggested moving here." With a flip of her hand she freed and loosened her hair, blonder, brighter than Anna remembered.

"I take it you're happy at The Studios."

"Oh, yes."

"And your dad?"

"Oh, he loves it, too."

County Highway B was winding through the spring-green woods, dampened here and there by creek runoff. Miniature waterfalls flowed out of banks close to the road and tree roots exposed themselves between eroded rows of stone like bad teeth in limestone gums.

Sebastian loves it, too.

At lunch, Heather's revelation about The Studios and St. Margaret made any other subject seem forced. Anna ate her tuna fish sandwich dutifully, inquiring now and then about Heather's classes at The Studios. She knew enough art history to broach a question or two about Renaissance art or Impressionism, but what could she say about algebra and geometry, much less trigonometry? Was that still the progression?

"I think you'll find Dad is a happier man than he used to be," Heather said, breaking through their thin conversation. Anna mouthed something positive, glad he was happy, et cetera, et cetera. Apparently he was happier now that he was no longer Anna's—say it—boyfriend. Her neighbors were right. Sebastian had never been anything more than a boyfriend. He'd known that. She hadn't.

Chapter Twenty-Nine

He was throwing a pot when Anna and Heather stepped into the single-story limestone building that housed the pottery studio. Looking up from the wheel, he smiled routinely before returning to the infant vessel wobbling in his hands. Broadening and narrowing it, urging the wet clay into a lip at the jar's mouth, he seemed unaware of anyone in the room, even the four students standing to one side of him during the demonstration.

"Want to see the painting studio while we wait?" Heather asked, already turning to leave. Anna, who had not seen Sebastian and his artistry for—how long had it been?—slowly followed.

Crossing gravel, they entered a glass-walled room in a newly built wood A-frame saturated with light. Resting on an easel among other easels scattered about the spacious room like patients waiting for appointments, Heather's still life glowed purple, a gathering of iris in a jar not unlike the one her father was making. Anna was struck by a sense of foreignness; separateness from both Heather and Sebastian. Here at The Studios she didn't speak the language.

Slightly nauseated by the thick, sweet smell of oils, she steadied herself against a tall stool while Heather, her eyes collecting light as richly as the iris collected purple, almost twirled from painting to painting. "Aren't they great?" she exclaimed. Anna imagined being able to twirl, able to escape Heather and Sebastian's changed lives and strange new setting. How glorious it would be to run again. To plunge into the green woods and never stop until she was back at The Oaks.

Of course, if she could run and twirl, she would not be living at The Oaks.

"They're lovely," said Anna.

"Do you want to see more of The Studios?"

"I'm happy for you, Heather, but I don't need to see more."

"Dad will be finished with his class soon."

"I'm ready to go home," said Anna. They both turned toward the door just as it opened.

"Hello, Anna."

Heather took Anna's arm and ushered the mute woman forward, less toward the door, Anna felt, than toward Sebastian.

"Care for some coffee?" he said.

Heather seemed to melt away, as if she were passing Anna off to someone who guided her out of the A-frame, back across gravel, and into the limestone building.

"You're looking well," Sebastian said when she'd stepped inside the studio once more. He pulled a rocking chair foward and picked up the large gray cat sleeping there. It landed on the floor, humped its back, and stalked to a corner. "Have a seat, Anna," Sebastian said, turning the cushion to its fresh side.

"I had no idea you were living in St. Margaret, Sebastian."

He lifted a battered coffeepot from a hot plate. "Why not? You made it clear you were finished with me." He rolled his desk chair nearer the rocker, then set their cups on a corner of the desktop. Seating himself, he leaned against the chair's scarred spindles and transferred his attention to Anna. His gaze focused her mind.

"We were interrupting each other's lives," she said.

"Heather and I were interrupting *yours*," he corrected.

"I think perhaps we're better off where we are, me at The Oaks and you and Heather—here. " Her face felt like a mask, her words like a script someone more poised than herself was reading from. Then, off-handedly, "How do you like teaching at The Studios?"

He'd been leaning toward her. At the rote question, he returned to the spindles without bothering to answer. "Why are you here, Anna?"

"Your daughter brought me. I had no idea we were coming to St. Margaret." *If I'd known, I wouldn't have come.* "Do you still have your apartment in town?"

"I sublet it."

Who would want to sublet a studio apartment in a warehouse basement, Sebastian? "Are you planning to move back to town, then?"

"Not soon," he said, "if ever. St. Margaret and The Studios are working out well for Heather."

"She seems happy," Anna murmured.

"She's better," he said. "We're both better."

"It was a good decision, then." Anna got to her feet. Before she'd taken two steps, the gray cat reclaimed the chair. *If these humans would just relax, skip the drama, I could shut down awareness and fall asleep again.* She envied cats.

"Sit down, Anna."

"I can't."

Sebastian scooped up the cat and set him on the floor a second time. A realist, the cat flexed his paws and settled into face-washing. "I'll be here as long as Heather is gaining confidence," Sebastian said.

Anna saw again how deeply committed he was. Almost alone, he'd made himself into a father. How different from her own experience as a girl and woman. She'd always wanted to be a wife and mother. Without effort she and Lorenzo had conceived Marianna. Two years later they lost her. A month after that, she lost Lorenzo. Since then she'd been almost as solitary as Sebastian. Yes, they were close, but over the years they'd become more of what they really were: a once-upon-a-time mother and a late, single father. A calm mother who had achieved peace with her sad memories; a distraught father seeking resolution for his assaulted daughter and for himself.

As she watched the untroubled cat, her relation to Sebastian came into focus: not just their many years together, but Heather's late entry into her father's life and, inevitably, her own. Heather, and now the assault, had changed everything.

"Is she still afraid?" Anna asked.

"Afraid of what?" Sebastian asked warily.

"Of life."

"She doesn't act afraid." He reached for his coffee but changed his mind. "She's going to testify against the guy."

"In Chicago?"

"Yeah. We're driving to Chicago next month." Folding his arms against himself, he said quietly, "She's more like her old self. Ready to make her mark."

"You've raised a strong daughter, Sebastian."

"At some point she'll leave me." His tone was fatalistic.

"Yes," Anna said, "but she needs you now."

His roof of forehead softened and his jaw came unclenched. "I've missed you, Anna."

"And I miss you, Sebastian." Though she sounded inaudible to herself, she saw by his face that he'd heard. She got to her feet again. The cat watched, narrow-eyed, before jumping back up into the rocker. He'd known all along the chair was his.

Driving Anna back to The Oaks, Heather was subdued. "How do you like The Studios?" she eventually asked.

"It's very nice," Anna said. "The woodsy setting is inspiring."

"It's a nice change for Dad."

Anna turned to look at Heather whose profile held steady against the dappled forest flashing by. "It seems to be a nice change for you, too." She paused. "Do you enjoy walking in the woods around The Studios? They're beautiful, aren't they." She was thinking about the basement apartment, the warehouse, its surrounding parking lot.

"I don't like the woods," Heather said.

Not like the woods? Anna would love nothing more than to walk, run, stand easily, for heaven's sake, in these woods. While she tried to frame a response, Heather was already talking.

"They're dark. You can't see what's behind you. Or in front of you, for that matter."

"You're used to an enclosed space," Anna suggested.

"I like my dorm room. The painting studio. The library. Yes, you could say I like enclosed spaces." She glanced at the gas gauge. "I wouldn't want to break down here in the woods." Then, without warning: "I have to testify against—"

"The trafficker?"

"The *rapist*." Heather landed hard on the word; assaulted the word. "He'll be in court. I'll have to look at him again." Her voice tightened. Her entire body tightened. "I have to tell the jury what he did."

"He'll be at the counsel table," Anna said, noncommittal. "With his attorney."

"Yes, and I'll be in the witness box and I'll have to see him."

"Your attorney has described the process to you?"

"Yes. He's not only *my* attorney, you know. There are several of us. This guy used more than just me..." She looked at Anna. "I guess you know what a trafficker is." Anna let Heather explain. "A trafficker captures someone and charges money to..."

"Exploit you. Sell you to buyers. It's courageous of you to testify, Heather."

"I dread coming back afterwards. To The Studios. Because of the woods." She thought for a moment. "Dad will be here. But I'll never step into a woods again."

Chapter Thirty

When Anna entered The Oaks dining room days later, she saw Michel sitting at Georgina and Orville's table. She'd heard he was recuperating from the heart attack, kidney failure, dialysis. Georgina waved and gestured for her to join them. When she reached their table, Michel smiled but did not stand.

"It's nice to see you, Michel," she said.

"Isn't he looking great?" Georgina gushed.

"He's indestructible!" Orville added. But Anna found it impossible to agree with them. Michel had lost weight. Bone and thinning hair showed the construction underlying his elegant face and head. His color was poor. He pulled the aluminum walker closer to his chair.

"Is this contraption in your way, Anna?"

"Not at all." Subdued, he waited for her to say something. She sat and glanced around the table. "It's been a long time since I've heard a word about Florida, Michel." It had also been a long time since she'd laughed outright. Michel was laughing, too.

"I'll try to remedy that," he said, and reached into his inner jacket pocket for a leather billfold which he opened to a photograph. "A friend recently sent me evidence of my old studio and showroom. It's still going strong." It did, indeed, seem to be going strong. Any doubt Anna held about his past success was dispelled by the sign above the door: *Michel's Sculptures.* "Here's one of my pieces." He pointed to a snowflake design hanging in the display window. "Copper."

"Excellent," said Anna.

"Brilliant!" said Georgina.

"You are too kind," Michel said insincerely. Slipping the billfold back inside his jacket, he asked, "How have you been, Anna?"

"Fine, Michel."

"And how is the young woman who went to Chicago?"

"Heather? You may recall that Chicago didn't work out. However, she's better now."

"And what is she doing?"

"Going to art school."

"Where?"

"St. Margaret."

He looked baffled.

"A small town about forty minutes from here."

"I see. And the school?"

"It's called The Studios."

"And her father?"

"He's teaching there. Pottery and welding."

"Versatile fellow."

"We didn't know he was teaching," Georgina said, speaking for herself and Orville who seemed more interested in his pancakes than in art or Sebastian.

"Will we be seeing him at The Oaks?" Michel asked.

"I don't think so."

"Not ever?" Georgina asked. "We'll miss him, won't we, Orville."

"I hardly ever saw him," said Orville.

"His daughter seems talented," said Michel. "Ambitious. I hope she's not showing her work in a gallery."

"Unless it's her own gallery." Anna's wry accommodation of Michel's opinion shocked her. She felt cynical.

"Can you join me for a drink this evening in the lounge?" he asked a little later, getting to his feet and leaning on the walker. She saw by his tremor that standing was an effort.

"Well, yes. Thank you."

"Five-thirty?"

"Five-thirty." His past contained cruelty. His future, like her own, was short. Nevertheless, at eighty years of age, Anna was still gripped by the present.

At five-thirty she came up behind him where he sat on the sofa they'd occupied that night weeks ago; the night Sebastian and Heather spotted them bent toward each other over drinks. The night Michel and Heather, out on the sunporch, had jumped to their feet and shouted at each other. In her memory, the fountain still splashed. Fireflies still knocked against the screens.

From the back, his shirt collar was careless and loose.

"Good evening," she said.

"You're looking well," he replied. One hand rested on the walker. The other touched an Oaks credit card lying on the low table in front of him. She sat down, positioning herself so she could see him face to face; could admire the wine-colored silk handkerchief in the jacket pocket and tasteful striped tie contrasting with the plain white shirt. *Two plain, one fancy,* he'd said to her once, describing his philosophy of dress. The philosophy still held. Except for the back of the collar he couldn't see.

"Would you do me a service, Anna?" He handed the card to her. "Would you order our drinks at the bar?"

"What would you like, Michel?"

"Bourbon. They'll remember." Anna went to the bar and came back with his bourbon and a sherry for herself.

"I've missed you, Anna."

"It's been a challenging few weeks for you," she said.

"Has it been only weeks? It seems like years." Inside his jacket, behind the brave handkerchief and tie, he seemed to sag. Just when she started to offer sympathy, he squared his frail shoulders and said, "Tell me: how is Sebastian?"

She took a swallow of sherry and waited for the sharp warmth to subside. "He seems to be happy in St. Margaret," she said. "He's teaching. He's near his daughter."

The bourbon remained on the table, untouched. "Does the girl still despise me?" Startled, Anna's mind spun back to the days when he'd talked constantly about himself and Florida. Was there to be no more of his self-centeredness? No more small talk? "Neither she nor her father can stand me," he said.

"Does that matter?"

"Only if it colors your opinion of me."

"My opinion is separate from theirs," she said. "I form my own opinions." He reached for his drink. Trembling, he spilled the bourbon. Looking more puzzled than chagrined, he set the glass back on the table. Anna imagined herself reaching for the drink and holding it to his mouth. She forced herself not to help.

"I have an opinion or two of my own," he said. She waited for the next slow sentence. "You may recall my sister."

"I remember her."

"I neglected Angelique," he said. Now Anna *did* help. She picked up the glass of bourbon and put it in his hand. "I'm a selfish man," he said, looking into the drink. "I wouldn't blame you if you agreed with Sebastian and his daughter."

"I despise any mistreatment of your sister," Anna said. "Of any woman. I despise when men feel entitled to women."

He looked up at her. "I don't feel entitled to you, Anna."

What if you were young and well, Michel? Or what if you could make money by selling me?

"Have I offended you again, Anna?"

She laid her hand on his forearm, thin inside the sleeve. "No, Michel." She weighed her words. "Your past offends me, not your present."

"When I look back, the court matter represents just a few short years in my life."

"The court matter, Michel, represents a grave crime against women."

He managed a swallow of his drink. "I've been assaulted myself, Anna." His eyes watered. Was it the sting of the bourbon? She listened to this once-quick man who could no longer pick up a glass without spilling. "I've been assaulted by old age and illness."

"We're all helpless against old age, Michel."

"Now I know."

"But we're not helpless against misuse," she said. "We have to fight that evil in others. Even more in ourselves." He was replying, but she had to lean closer to hear him. And she had to be patient.

"I always fought for my gallery. For buyers. For costs and prices." Though he sounded weak, Anna noted his fierce concentration. "I fought for money to keep making art. My studio wasn't always profitable, you know." He rested from speech.

"There is profit, and there is profit," she said.

"Go on, Anna."

"You neglected your sister," she said, keeping an eye on the sick old man. He was listening. "Now you're sorry. What about the women you trafficked?"

"I didn't personally traffic anyone," he objected. She thought he would have liked to stand and defend himself.

"Why were you incarcerated, Michel?"

He almost appeared to sit down again although he hadn't been standing. His gaze moved off her face and drifted loosely into empty space.

"Heather hasn't been assaulted by illness and old age, Michel. She's been assaulted by men. Violent men. She's been invaded and she can never fully recover from that." She felt she'd said more than he could absorb. He stared into his lap, perhaps at his impotence.

He looked up. "I was very wrong." She felt no pity, no admiration, no contempt. "I've damaged women." Acknowledging it, he achieved a dignity she hadn't seen in him before. He wiped his eyes with a white handkerchief—clean and monogrammed—from a pocket reached with difficulty. Anna sat quite still and offered no condolence. Every now and then she helped him pick up the glass of bourbon from the table.

Chapter Thirty-One

"Your father didn't tell me you were leaving for Chicago," Anna complained two weeks later. "Neither of you told me." She resented being involved in the Chicago trauma months earlier, yet kept ignorant of the trial a week ago.

"We didn't want to trouble you," Heather said over coffee and cinnamon rolls at Anna's kitchen bar.

"Didn't want to trouble me! I've been troubled since the day you were assaulted!"

Heather looked shocked at the outburst. "Dad and I didn't realize..." She trailed off.

"You were both terribly upset, Heather. I know that. But so was I."

"We didn't know. You didn't tell us."

"Your father knew."

Heather picked up a piece of pastry with her fingers but put it down again. "Is that why things changed between you?"

Anna looked up from where she'd been watching the midmorning light come closer and closer to the blue ceramic jars lined up on the counter—cookies, flour, sugar. "I decided not to see your dad anymore."

"I'm sorry," Heather said after a lengthy silence. "Did you break up because of me?"

"Not because of anything you did," Anna said. "Or anything that was done to you."

"Dad is private," Heather said. "He didn't tell me you broke up. I just noticed it for myself."

"He is very private," Anna agreed. "He doesn't like it when people know what he's thinking."

"He doesn't like being told what to do," Heather said.

"He won't risk—"

"Won't risk what?"

"Criticism. Or sympathy. An offer of help."

"What does he need help with?"

Anna took a breath. "He raised you alone when he could have shared responsibility. He could have made it easier on himself."

"Dad doesn't need help. He's a great father."

Anna's face must have shown skepticism.

"He believes in himself and he believes in me."

"But in Chicago—"

"He doesn't tell me what to do," Heather insisted. "He doesn't tell you what to do, either, does he?"

"No, he doesn't."

"And you like that, don't you?"

"Yes."

"Well, so do I."

"But in Chicago—"

Heather stepped down from the high kitchen stool. "It's not Dad's fault! That could happen to anyone! There were four plaintiffs at the trial and plenty of others who wouldn't testify."

"It took courage to testify," Anna conceded.

"You bet it did!" Heather took her cup and rinsed it at the sink. "The guy didn't look like the same person," she said over her shoulder. "He looked nice. He was in a business suit. But I knew him. I knew the man under the suit." She turned sharply. "How could Dad have prevented what happened?" She braced herself against the sink. "It's not his fault that some men are sex addicts and predators and rapists."

"No, it's not."

"Then why are you criticizing him?"

"He could have paid attention to what you were doing on the computer. On the internet."

"But that would be invading my privacy."

"I see."

"It's not Dad's style."

"That's true."

"He doesn't invade *your* privacy, does he?"

"No, he doesn't. When he spent time at my house on Woodland Street, it wasn't an invasion. I welcomed him."

"Yeah," Heather said, her eyes bright, her face heated.

"And I washed his socks and pajamas and underwear because I wanted to."

"If you hadn't wanted to, you wouldn't have."

"And I understood when he wanted a child and went outside our relationship to create—you."

"Because you were too old to have a baby."

"True."

"Dad didn't blame you for not getting pregnant, did he?"

"No, he didn't. He's a realist."

"So how can you say he's not a good father?"

"He could have taught you about the damage some men are capable of."

"Dad didn't damage *you*, did he?"

"Never. He made me happy."

"He treated you well."

"Yes, he did."

"Then why are you criticizing him?"

"Because he didn't tell you about the possible dangers of arousing a man's interest. Or the possible danger to you when a man arouses *you*."

"I wasn't aroused! I was attracted to his art gallery!"

"And he was attracted to selling you."

"It won't ever happen to me again."

"I hope not, Heather. I hope it never happens to anyone."

"Because I'm never going to have a boyfriend."

"All right."

"I'm never going to have sex. It's the furthest thing from my mind."

"Not mine," said Anna. "I miss your father."

"You should just forget him, Anna."

"I'll try," Anna said. "I'll try, Heather."

Chapter Thirty-Two

Two weeks later Heather called again. "Can I pick you up at The Oaks tomorrow? We can eat at Duck's Cafe like we did last time."

"How about eating in town?"

"Well, I enjoy the drive."

"In the woods?"

Anna's land line went silent for a moment. "Dad wants to see you."

"Why doesn't he drive to town himself?"

"He doesn't know if you want to see him."

Now the silence was Anna's. "So we'll be driving on to The Studios after lunch?"

"Yes. And you'll be driven back to The Oaks afterwards."

Anna was puzzled. Was Sebastian protecting himself from rejection? Was Heather acting out a courtship for her father she claimed she would never perform for herself? Anna was ashamed of a nasty thought: *is she pimping for her father?* Or perhaps Sebastian was rethinking his relationship to an aging woman who now lived in a retirement center instead of a comfortable home of her own on Woodland Street. An old woman who might need care in the next few years and who might, after all, be worth the trouble. *If we really want to live separate lives,* she thought, *this is the time to do it.*

"Anna?"

"Yes, I'll have lunch with you tomorrow."

"And you'll come to The Studios?"

"I'll be happy to go."

"It's strange," Heather said the next day on the way to St. Margaret. "I like my correspondence courses a lot. Art history, for instance. It's fascinating. And history. General science, too. Of course, my favorite class is still painting. I'm having a lot of success in the studio."

"I'd like to see what you're working on," Anna said, taking an interest in this trip through the woods now that she knew Sebastian wanted to see her. Shafts of summer sunlight penetrated sycamore along the road. She glanced sideways at the gas gauge.

"I filled up in town," Heather said, adding, "sorry the air conditioner doesn't work."

Heat did not bother Anna as it used to. Sensations of all kinds were less intense than they used to be. She experienced fewer minor annoyances. She made fewer judgements about people. Spent less time noting heart palpitations, random headaches, arthritic thumbs. She didn't miss sex as much as she used to. With one finger she wiped slight perspiration from her upper lip and turned back to the woods.

"We'll visit the painting studio first," Heather said, "and then we'll see Dad." But when they'd parked in front of the pottery studio, Sebastian appeared almost immediately, nearly as tall as the limestone doorway and lintel of the old building. He approached the passenger side of the Plymouth.

"How are you, Anna?" Opening the door, he offered his hand. The strength she leaned on was steadying, yet their closeness nearly gave her vertigo. They had wasted so much time apart.

"Shall we look at Heather's work before we have coffee?" Inside the painting studio, easels still stood in their semi-circle, alive and patient. A self-portrait stared out from Heather's canvas. Bleak face. Neckline of bright orange sweater slashing the lower half of the picture space. Straight-line lips. Nose without definition. Vacant eyes. Behind the face and head, overpowering swarm of wallpaper.

I like the wallpaper, Anna thought to herself. "I miss the energy and vigor in your face," she said aloud.

"I can't always be vigorous," Heather retorted.

"No, I suppose none of us can." While she viewed other paintings, Sebastian moved toward the door. Minutes later he and Anna were crossing the scrawny strip of summer grass and sun-whitened gravel between buildings. Under the weight of their past together, and of the July heat, and of the heavy woods surrounding them, both of them were silent. The cat still dozed in the rocking chair beside the desk, dropping tidily to the floor when Sebastian scooped him off the cushion. Anna sat down and waited while Sebastian made fresh coffee at the hot plate.

"Heather wasn't sure you'd be willing to come out to St. Margaret again," he said. "I wasn't sure, either."

"I gave it some thought," Anna said. They eyed each other without particular warmth.

Neither confident nor needy, she'd never felt calmer. Freer. Without compulsion. Sebastian's wiry hair was grayer than she remembered, but his eyes were as observant and penetrating as ever. The air between them was cool, not from the air conditioning, but from awareness;

self-awareness and awareness of each other. They might have been in some kind of negotiation.

"I've missed you, Anna."

"And I've missed you, Sebastian."

"I'm not as preoccupied with my daughter as I was."

"She seems to be enjoying The Studios," Anna said. "She's maturing."

"You would have admired her at the trial. Her testimony was very effective."

"I wish you'd told me you were going for the trial."

"It was not something you needed to know, Anna."

"But I *did* need to know. You didn't hesitate to tell me about the assault. You called me while you were still on the Interstate. You involved me from the beginning." Their abstract calm disintegrated. He stood and warmed their coffee cups from the pot on the hot plate. "And then you pulled away from me." Resentment darkened her voice.

"What do you want me to say, Anna?"

She had words, but they wouldn't be his words. Slowly he came back to the desk and sat down in his spindle chair. "I'd like to start over again."

"With me?"

"Yes. Heather is better now. So am I." He leaned forward and took her hand. "I needed time to think. Now I'm clear again."

"What are you clear about?"

But he had nothing more to say.

"I wish you could explain yourself to me," she said, realizing that he felt no need to. He had already answered. Perhaps her questions helped him retain the privacy that was his second nature. "Do you want me to stop trying to understand you?"

"I want you to trust me," he said.

"I trust you to be yourself, Sebastian."

He softened and leaned forward. "I trust you, too, Anna. I've loved you for years." He sat back. "May I drive you home?"

"Yes, Sebastian. You may drive me home."

And so they rode back to The Oaks, Sebastian driving Heather's car. He dropped her off by the entrance and parked the car. Dinner would be served in the dining room at five-thirty, as usual. Upstairs she poured out wine, a juice glass for him, a wine glass for her. They sat quietly before going downstairs. At five-thirty, Georgina and Orville joined them at their table, more sedate than usual, as if they respected Anna and Sebastian's privacy. Several tables over, Michel ate with three women, entertaining them with less gusto than in the past, but still able to amuse.

Returning upstairs, Anna and Sebastian sat on the sofa in the den and watched the evening news without interest. Sebastian took her hand. "Can we go to bed early?"

"Yes," she said, and rested her head on his shoulder.

"Have you thrown out my clean socks?"

"Never," she said. They smiled. Turning off the television, they went into the bedroom, taking turns in the bathroom as they had always done, slipping into bed one at a time. As was his habit, Sebastian lay on his back and felt for Anna's hand. She liked curling up against him, sensing him in the dark, feeling his hearbeat when he drew her hand onto his chest. And slowly he, too, turned and together they nursed their relationship, paying attention to their old habits and to what each of them liked. Soon they abandoned thought and welcomed the lust that slowly built, lust mingled with love that they knew well how to indulge and control.

About the Author

When she's not reading, playing the piano, or talking to other writers, Marlene Lee holds down a table at a local coffee house in Columbia, Missouri, confronting blank pages during business hours and postponing the inevitable with another cup of coffee.

Before her freelance court reporting career, she taught high school English, children's special education, Freshman and Sophomore college English, and vocational classes in stenotype. Always and in-between, she wrote short stories and novels, accumulating publishable manuscripts before being actually published in 2013. (Lee's earlier fiction titles: *The Absent Woman, Rebecca's Road, Scoville, Limestone Wall, No Certain Home,* and *Inner Passage, Collected Short Stories.*)

Printed in the USA
CPSIA information can be obtained
at www.ICGtesting.com
JSHW080218130724
66229JS00002B/14